MAN ON THE STREET

Melissa J

ISBN: 1490551743
ISBN 13: 9781490551746

CHAPTER 1

THE MARCH OF DIMES

They say everybody's got a right to be their own way. At the same time, I got a right to think that everybody sucks.

The fresh, winter air was stone cold, biting my nuts as I opened the door of my apartment. I hustled down the stairs of my building in an attempt to warm up. It wasn't working so I started running even faster. As soon as I got to the bottom of the steps, I slammed into the person who had been lurking at the base of the stairs.

I wasn't looking for trouble that morning, but it found me. I had seen the kid around before, and he was nothing but a piece of shit in my eyes.

"Bam," I said under my breath after colliding with him. That's what people say these days, "bam."

The head-on collision made me feel like a football player. I backpedaled for a second but stayed on my feet. Slamming into someone is always an odd situation; this time was no different. The impact had forced hot air out of his jacket. It felt good for a second on my cold face, reminding me of when the door of the boiler room is propped open. It wasn't much to get excited about, but free heat is like a free cookie; you take what you can get.

I looked into his crossed and bloodshot eyes, under his mop of wavy, red hair. I hate red-heads and I hate homeless people. This kid was pissing me off just being alive. Although, while I was in the middle of studying his scabs and smelling the medley of urine and feces that he was wearing like cologne, it occurred to me that every homeless person is like an abandoned building in a sense. Behind all of the broken windows and boarded-up doors, there is damage beyond description and a series of repairs no handyman could fix.

The homeless kid and I stood there for a moment.

I tried apologizing, but he just stared back at me blankly. I could see my words were not taking root in his brain, and I thought about hitting him because of the hair, but I had a bus to catch, so I just kept moving. Fuck him.

I walked swiftly through the courtyard of my apartment complex and onto the filthy city street. Bits of trash were sticking to the sidewalk like wallpaper, and I had to pry my feet from the ground with every step I took. It was like walking around in a movie theater that had an old layer of popcorn butter spackled all over the floor. I wouldn't be calming down anytime soon.

As I walked, I wondered about what was wrong with the red-headed kid. It had to be something. Perhaps his life could have turned out normal, but maybe society screwed him up, and he found himself staggering around city streets, living the only life he knew.

I laughed to myself. I knew better.

In reality, the kid was probably just an asshole with some serious mental imbalances and no house. I don't sympathize with people who stagger around apartment buildings early in the morning for one simple reason: they're all fucked in the head.

I do have a little bit of sympathy for red-headed kids. Every red-head I see reminds me of the character Malachai from *Children of the Corn*. Of course, not that many people these days have seen that movie, so nobody gets that joke. It's weird when time passes.

My name is Manny Crocker, and I will never let them see my hair. I've been wearing a hat for so long that sometimes I even forget what color my own hair is. I stand tall, at six feet, three inches, and I have never once worn a tie in my entire life. I'm a twenty-four year old man and I'm single.

The outskirts of Philadelphia, the parts the tourists will never see, have been home to me for my entire life, but none of that matters. The only thing you need to remember about me is I don't give a fuck.

I awoke this morning with the knowledge that my father had stolen a loaded handgun from my apartment, along with the first twenty-four years of my life. He said that he didn't take the gun, but I knew he did.

Yesterday I had come home from the Laundromat with a bag of wet clothes by my side. The clothes were supposed to be dry, but that's another story.

While I was opening the door to my apartment, I could feel a presence, as if someone had just been inside my home. It was as though I could still smell a spiritual belch that someone had left behind, lingering in the air. Don't get me wrong; I'm not into all that new-age, cosmic bullshit, but I can tell when someone's been in my house.

Panicking, I went down the list of things that needed to be in the right place: cash, stash, and gun. When I got to door number three, I knew I had been robbed. I quickly scanned the windows and doors of the apartment for any obvious signs of a break-in, but all the seals were clean.

I knew immediately that my dad was the one who had taken my gun. I had forgotten my jacket, with the keys in the pocket, at his place a few months ago. I knew my dad took my keys at the time and copied them. There was no doubt in my mind that he used the key to get to my gun, and I knew exactly where the stolen booty would be in his house. When I called him later to confront him about it, he sounded distressed in a way I had never heard before. It was strange to hear the man who raised me acting so scared.

Dad never admitted to me he had the gun. He just told me to shove it.

This situation would get a lot worse before it got any better.

I have always hated winter, and that morning was no different. March in the city of Philadelphia was bitterly cold. I walked in silence to the bus stop. Every time I looked up to see the outside world, it only made me wish I had stayed inside. The biting wind smacked my face along the way. I wanted to be inside every house, apartment, and coffee shop I saw, one at a time.

The rest of the nation doesn't think of Philadelphia as being a cold city. They call us "The City of Brotherly Love." Personally, I want our city to get one of the better and tougher names such as "The Steel City" or "The Windy City." Instead, we're stuck with man-on-man imagery. Who's making love to his brother around here, anyway?

My body twitched as I continued walking toward the prison that society refers to as "public transportation." I began fantasizing about a limousine, full of hookers serving hot soup, with the heat pumping at full blast. The concept seemed like a miracle on a day as cold as that, like turning water into wine.

Every winter, the national television stations run stories about the blight of the poor people in Detroit and Chicago, but nobody cares about how cold it is for the people stuck in Philadelphia, and anyone who's from here will tell you that. I think it gets a little colder in this city than in those other places because we don't get any credit for it.

Last night I ran out of change at the Laundromat, and I couldn't finish drying my clothes; they were still damp, and it sucked big time. I had the money to finish the job, but the machine that makes change was out. That pissed me off . . . greatly.

I wanted to ask around for help, but I hate the people at the Laundromat who run out of quarters then beg for them. They're pathetic.

I wished I could be at home, smoking weed and watching TV. Stumbling down a city street like a zombie in wet clothes is a bad idea, but it's hard to relax when a loaded handgun, registered in your name, walks out of your house. The smart move is to follow it.

I arrived at the bus stop and joined the peanut gallery of lowlifes slowly assembling there. As I dug through my pocket for bus fare, I found a half-smoked joint I had forgotten about from the night before. Breakfast.

I quickly lit up the magic stick while hiding it under my jacket. The smoke tasted great, but the irony was bitter. Sneaking a smoke in public reminded me of Ralph, one of my best friends from high school. He recently ripped me off on a six-hundred-dollar football bet and a quarter ounce of some of the juiciest and most expensive smoke out there. The smell of the herb prompted me that I needed to kick his ass, too.

While sitting on the bench, I pictured several scenarios where I confronted Ralph then kicked the crap out of him while I poetically explained the difference between right and wrong. Everyone has those fantasies. I should have known better than to cover him on that bet. The word was all over town that Ralph's life was going south, and it was all over his face in the weeks before he left town. He had given up.

I knew from experience that the immediate problem with my dad would be like popping a zit; blood would spill, but then it would be over, one way or another. On the other hand, my problems with Ralph were only getting started. Pops had my gun, and I would get it back, but Ralph didn't have my money. I would've had a much fatter and fresher joint if he did. Collecting from him would be more difficult.

After sitting on the bench at the bus stop for several meaningless minutes of boredom, the bus arrived. I sleepily boarded, found a seat in the back, and pressed my face as close to the window as I could without touching it. Time slowly passed along with the scenery. I started to forget about things as the smell of cheap plastic upholstery filled my nose.

It was my birthday, and my parents were taking me to the store to buy a baseball glove. I sat in the back of the car, my face pressed as close to the window as I could without touching it.

All day, my dad had been yelling at me because I wouldn't stop fidgeting with the collar of my shirt. Being a nervous kid, I neurotically pulled on the shirt neck whenever anyone talked to me. Needless to say, my whole little-kid wardrobe had turned into V-necks, driving my father crazy. It didn't help that anytime he tried to talk to me about it, I would get anxious and fidget with the neck of my shirt. I guess it was pretty annoying when he was talking to me about a habit that needed changing, and I would engage in that very habit before the conversation ended.

As soon as I got in the car, the excitement of my birthday piqued my nerves.

Suddenly my face spun around almost 180 degrees. I recoiled in pain. For a second, I thought we'd had a car accident, but we kept getting into accidents with increasing strength and frequency. Slowly I realized I was being hit.

"Stop it! We're in public," the woman in the front screamed at the man. "Not now. There's people around."

"Shut the fuck up or you're next."

"You wouldn't dare do anything in public." The woman spoke defiantly, but she was sobbing. "You wouldn't dare."

They continued to yell at each other in the front seat until he hit her. It felt good to not be getting hit.

Bam! After hearing the noise, I felt the pain, lots of pain. My face felt shattered. I sat up straight and somehow managed to open my eyes, shivering and slowly realizing what had just happened.

The bus had dipped into a pothole and jerked me around in my seat, causing the window to pound me square on the nose. My face felt like one big nerve ending. The pain shot through my face and jaw like angry lightning.

I ride the bus every goddamned day, and I have mastered the art of falling asleep in my seat while sitting up perfectly straight. The hum of the large engine makes falling asleep on the bus as easy as farting after a bowl of beans. The downfall of sleeping on the bus is that, once in a while, the bus slams into a pothole and I end up feeling like a golf ball on a Saturday morning.

It was a tough way to come out of a dream, but it didn't matter. Life is harsh. Waking up to it is no different. I straightened my back and rubbed my nose.

Sharp pains from indigestion burned through my stomach as I shook the cobwebs out of my head. I thought about the upcoming violence I would face when the ride ended. Riding the bus was supposed to be the peaceful part of the morning, but it sure as hell wasn't today.

The crowded bus felt like a gigantic, metal coffin, ushering well-dressed corpses to an early grave. I looked around at the other people riding the bus, going to work.

A guy sitting next to me stayed so engrossed in the *New York Times* crossword puzzle, it was as though the fate of the world depended on his ability to solve it. For him, it did.

I wondered why the problems in these people's lives weren't anything close to the problems in my life. I knew that when the ride ended, we would all go our separate ways. That fact made me want to stay on the bus.

I glanced again at the guy doing the crossword puzzle. As I wondered about where both of us would be in twenty years, an ominous feeling surrounded me, like the stench of a bean fart.

After the bus had hit the ditch that kicked my ass, we crawled through traffic. We idled for what seemed a long time. The minutes turn into hours when you're trying to get somewhere as quickly as possible. The bus could have made the right turn if the driver of the car in front of us weren't too much of a pussy to force his way into the throng of jaywalkers dancing in the streets. The result was the pedestrian gang-bang in front of me that had been going on for several lights now. We couldn't turn.

The ethical dilemma in front of us was that the pedestrians wouldn't stop crowding the crosswalk when the big hand told them it was time to stop. Sometimes people don't follow the rules. The people in the back of the bus were on their feet, yelling at the car in front of us. I was one of them. The scene reminded me of being in a movie theater with some jerk who won't sit down.

The bus sucks. It smells bad and they don't serve food or coffee. I'd been to jail before, and it didn't smell much worse in there. Despite the lack of sundries, my eyes managed to shut themselves once more.

As I slept on the bus, I drifted toward another birthday maybe two years later.

My birthday always got my dad angry, every single year. A birthday is supposed to be a celebration of your life and the sponsors who make it all possible—*supposed* to be. I always dreaded occasions that forced us to turn a flood light on things that we were not. Trying to celebrate a holiday in an abusive home is like giving a microscope to a leper.

All week my dad had been dropping hints that I would be getting a bike for my birthday. He seemed more eager about it than I was. I think it might have been the mental image of my rolling in a direction away from him, but whatever the reason, getting my first bike marked a huge milestone in my young life.

We slid into the car and headed out of our neighborhood, two men on a mission. My dad tousled my hair, something he did rarely.

It seemed to take a long time to get to the store, and I got restless in the front seat. I wanted my bike. Time assumes a completely different dimension when you're a little kid who wants something.

We continued driving around in random suburban neighborhoods for several more hours, despite my persistent questioning about where we were going. I thought it was strange that we weren't at the mall.

As I watched the sun sink in the sky, I realized I wouldn't be spending the afternoon of my birthday riding a brand-new, store-bought bicycle. When we left the house earlier, it was a warm but breezy afternoon; all I had on was a T-shirt and jeans. The darkening sky made for a cold evening, raising goose bumps on my arms. And we hadn't eaten dinner. My head started to hurt.

Periodically my dad would park on the street and leave me alone in the car for several minutes. After returning in frustration, he would tell me he couldn't find the store.

"Why is this store in a neighborhood? How come there's no parking lot here?" I kept asking my dad. "At the mall they have a parking lot, and you can see the store from the parking lot." My questions fell on deaf ears.

When it got too dark to see, my dad parked the car and disappeared again. I waited in the car. Suddenly I heard people yelling.

I turned around to see my dad running down the street toward the car.

He arrived quickly and angrily wrestled an enormous metal object, which smelled like pavement, into the back seat of the car. He tried furiously to close the door, but it wasn't working. The steel sculpture was hard to recognize, wedged into the car as it was.

I heard shouts from an angry mob forming in the distance.

Although it was upside down and hanging out of the open door, I soon recognized the metallic chunk in the back seat: a bike with worn-down tires and no price tags like the ones they sell at the mall.

With one final shove, my dad got his catch into the car. As soon as he could get himself behind the wheel and the key turned, the car exploded forward and we drove off, despite the back door's still being open.

I turned around again at a pounding noise. Two men were running as fast as they could after the car. The bigger of the two had his hand on the open door, pounding on the side of the car. The other tried to keep up while yelling and throwing rocks at the bumper.

This time there was no woman sitting in the car or waiting at the house.

The car snapped into a higher gear, and the angry men fell away. The bike stayed inside the car, and we made our escape.

I felt bad for them because they wanted to chase the car, but they had no bike.

"Who are those men chasing after us?" I asked.

My dad cleared his throat several times before stuttering on his words. "Some . . . friends of mine."

"Why are they chasing us?"

Catching his breath, Dad answered with confidence the second time. "It's like this, kid: We're all playing a big game of tag." He panted a few more times as he looked in the rearview mirror. He spoke through his clenched teeth. "And now . . . they're it."

Falling asleep on the bus sucks. To make matters worse, you have to wake up on the bus. I never liked waking up. A man waking up is a stranger to himself. As the eyes break their morning seal, the first sense of familiarity kicks in, and a person's life story flashes before his bloodshot eyes.

Waking up and getting acquainted with yourself can be a good thing if you're somebody cool, such as Mike D from the Beastie Boys, or a bad thing if you're some jack-off like me with a bunch of debts and no Laundromat change.

While I was awakening on the bus, I became painfully aware of the mundanity of my existence. I was a resident of the state of Pennsylvania, living in the city of Philadelphia, riding a public bus to Camden, New Jersey, where I wasn't sure how things were going to turn out. I remembered it was Thursday and I was single. It wasn't much to wake up to, but none of it mattered. Without John Belushi, the whole world sucked anyway.

Scratching my head, I thought about Ralph. He and I were going to have a confrontation; I didn't know when, but it would happen. I would not let him screw me out of my money. He had been spotted working at a hamburger joint about twenty-five minutes from where I live. Great. More time on the bus. I laughed to myself. Ralph thought he could just switch up neighborhoods to avoid me? The waitresses around here were like a spy network.

Ralph might have been able to stay in the neighborhood and still avoid me, but I wasn't the only one he owed money to. Ralph's entire life had gone south. He needed a place to hide and an hourly job so he wouldn't starve. He knew we didn't circulate in his new neighborhood, but we didn't have to. Becky, the talkative waitress at our diner, lived there.

A few nights ago, John and I were sitting in a booth at our regular diner, impatiently awaiting our overdue waitress. Finally Becky strolled up to our table and blew our minds.

"I saw your friend Ralph working at the Happy Burger by my apartment the other day."

Ralph had turned into the great white whale: several had seen him but no one could land him. We were dumbfounded that Becky had revealed a place he would be sure to return to on a regular basis. Better yet, it was publicly accessible. We looked at her blankly.

She spoke with a tone that was firm and assertive, yet polite enough not to hurt her tip. It was a timeless dance. "I went in to eat with my sister, and I saw him in there last week. He was flippin' burgers behind the grill," she said confidently, the gum in her mouth accenting her speech with little pops. "Now what can I get—?"

The words hadn't even finished rolling off her tongue before both of us had grabbed her by the arms, firmly but politely. John and I were seeking long-awaited answers. Becky knew something about Ralph, the deadbeat, and both of us wanted to get to him . . . first.

It was an odd scene at that point, a Philly waitress with her hair tucked up in a bun and identical street hustlers hanging off each arm. Realizing at the exact same moment we were overreacting, we released her immediately. The three of us looked squarely at one another for a moment. Then we got down to business.

I walked down the street, getting slower and slower until I finally stopped, steeping in the reality of my situation. The scene at the diner had been replaying in my head like some movie. The problem for me was that while I had been spacing out, I had stopped paying attention. Now I had no clue where I was.

The bus had dropped me off in Camden, and I had just started walking. I looked around and realized my feet had taken me to the avenue of my adolescence.

The streets resembled the overcrowded shelves of a convenience store pretending to be a grocery store: cans of minestrone soup facing off menacingly with boxes of rice, cereal boxes smelling like taco powder, and coffee tasting like garlic. Picture a supermarket without parking and without enough food for every customer; that's probably the best way to describe where I'm from. Aside from that, the neighborhood was nothing more than streets full of houses that could all use a fresh coat of paint. After all of this time, my father still lived here. I needed to stop drifting off in my head. I couldn't believe I had subconsciously come to this place.

The rest of my life would have its own set of problems and bullshit, but for right now, it was morning outside the City of Brotherly Love, and my gun was missing.

I heard a car start in the distance, and it made me think about the neighbors. "Keep your friends close but your enemies closer." Whoever wrote that must have known our neighbor Ron Sanchez.

Ron always stared at my forehead, much to my dismay. He would study my cranium while picking at his gold teeth with his ubiquitous toothpick. Any time I saw him, I felt the answers to life's mysteries were written on my forehead.

I never cared much for his gold teeth, either. I always thought it would be funny to spell out something in diamonds on his teeth, perhaps *High Profile* or *Cocaine*. Gold teeth aren't something you see every day; they never got into the mainstream fashion because all of the moguls who pioneered the look ended up in jail. The bottom line is people with gold teeth get their cars searched.

My dad hated Ron with a passion. Every single day, my dad would open the door and look around to see Ron's Mexican flag flying right in his face. The smell of his wife's spicy cooking filled the air, and their porch was crowded with plants the same way their house was crowded with people.

Their lifestyle was a little loud, but part of living in low-income housing is that sometimes your front yard turns into a billboard for some foreign culture. Don't get me wrong; people who looked and smelled different didn't really bother me either way. I just didn't care. But for my dad, their culture was the kind of slap in the face that he refused to accept. Over the next twenty years, he would marinate his hatred daily in the melting pot that we call America.

"Look at this shit," he would say. "They should get jerseys that say *Wetback #1* and *Wetback #2*." He paused to carefully craft his next comment.

"Better yet, they should stick to track, like when the border patrol is chasing them."

As his son, I assumed I was supposed to echo his comments, but I was unable to do so. Every young boy tries to keep his parents happy, but my attempts were unsuccessful. I just didn't have the passion for hating minorities that he did. He was the only person who ever did bad things to me, and he was white. I didn't get it.

He continued hand-cranking the engine of hatred, which periodically sputtered out his off-tempo monologue. The veins in his eyes reflected the fingers of sunlight that sneaked into the room between the open blinds. The lines on his temples looked like dried-out riverbeds.

I gazed outside at Ron playing ball with his son Juan. In my entire life, I never once played sports or went to the park with my dad. I wanted to be out of the house so badly, but I was too young to go out on my own. Out on the street, it was a warm, Sunday afternoon, but inside it was a different story.

"He's trying to throw a football? That's an American sport. Look at him! What's his name? Hulia or Huna or something?"

I knew my dad expected me to reply to his many questions and comments, but I had grown silent after a few minutes and just sat there. As my replies tapered off, I could see him getting upset.

Despite my dad's enthusiasm, the truth at that point in my life was that Juan Sanchez, the filthy, little wetback he was referring to, was the only friend I had in the entire world. Much like my dad, I'd also come to hate Ron Sanchez, although it was for completely different reasons, but Juan Sanchez was my best friend from day one.

I stood frozen in my tracks, like a lamppost on the street. I was about one hundred yards from the set, and the flood of memories refused to stop.

—⚡—

The first time I met Juan Sanchez was in the bathroom of our grade school. I was in the third grade, and he was in the first.

When I entered the restroom, I saw Juan leaning over the sink with his shirt off, splashing cold water on his back. As I got closer to him, I saw bloody welts and belt marks on his back, the florescent light glistening off the raw skin that was exposed.

Suddenly Juan looked up at me in embarrassment. He put his shirt on immediately and left hurriedly. No words were spoken that morning in the bathroom, but that's when our friendship began.

Our introduction was uncommon among little kids, to say the least. Normally, when two children come together around a football or a fire truck, there is a lot of talking going on between them. Two little kids meeting at a back full of welts is a completely different story.

That morning in the bathroom, I discovered a completely different understanding of my neighbor Juan, unlike the one being presented at home. We were like blood brothers in an extended abusive family. Despite our separate-but-equal racist upbringings, both of us knew that morning that we were the same. Sometimes the greatest communications are completely silent.

—⚡—

At that moment my heart started pounding like a jackhammer, and I knew I needed to live the life that was in front of me, not the one in my imagination.

I had been daydreaming on the wrong block in the wrong neighborhood, avoiding the facts in front of me. There would be plenty of time to think about Ron and his gold teeth on the bus. Prancing around in a neighborhood such as this makes you a target.

I grew up in this neighborhood, but that didn't mean shit because the new kids on the block didn't know me, and they would stick me even if they did.

Some ghettos are famous, but it's the ones you've never heard about that will bite you in the ass. The average person knows you're not supposed to walk around in South Central Los Angeles because a whole generation of rappers spent a decade talking about what a tough place it is. Nobody got rich rapping about Camden, New Jersey, and nobody in the top forty is telling you to hide your shit around here. This place is the real deal.

All I wanted was to get my gun back and get the hell out. I guess sometimes happiness is a warm gun.

Maybe I was just stoned; maybe I wanted to avoid doing this, but once again my mind took a walk. I heard the echo of my teenage voice, bouncing around on the concrete stage. The neighborhood had once again forced me to relive something I wanted to forget.

———

It was a Friday night. A group of us had gathered at my friend Zach's house to watch movies. None of us were savvy enough to get our hands on any drugs or alcohol, but all the same, the last remains of childhood innocence hung in the air like Christmas decorations in January. Movies and popcorn, a pastime that was moments away from obscurity, were the focus of our Friday-night party.

A Clockwork Orange was playing on the TV. The scene when the lady gets raped in the old-fashioned theater came on. I was having a conversation with one of my friends about which girl had the biggest jugs in our junior high school when the sound of the woman's screams began grating on my ears. Her distant cries felt like razor blades on the side of my face, and my focus turned to the screen.

I watched silently and received my Hollywood baptism into the world of forced and violent sex. The woman's detached screams reverberated on the cheap speakers, sucking me back to an event that happened eight years before that night. The incident had been repressed from my memory until the sound of the actress unleashed it like a hungry dragon.

On the night in question, a friend was staying over. I never saw Sam again after that night. It's not surprising, considering what happened.

I must have been around three years old at the time. Since I wasn't getting much attention at home, I was fired up to have my first partner in crime, so to speak. Sam and I pretended to be professional wrestlers almost the entire night, much to my father's dismay, as shown by his yelling at us to stop. Eventually the grown-ups went to bed, but the kids stayed up to party down. Falling asleep is not what a slumber party is about. The big people never understood the facts.

Sam and I slipped out of bed and escaped to the freedom of the hallway. We were sliding around on the floor, making humming engine noises like two racecars. We cruised to the end of the hallway and romped around together by my parents' bedroom door until someone grabbed me.

Sam was pulling me away from my parents' door. He sat me down about five feet from the door, just far enough so if the door swung open, it wouldn't launch me like a hockey puck.

He was scared but I didn't know why. I had gotten so distracted by my life as a racecar that I hadn't heard the screaming coming from the bedroom. He sat there with a horrified look on his face, afraid to move. The screaming continued. Before he went to bed, my dad had sternly warned us not to leave the bedroom, but this was a slumber party.

The woman's shrill and piercing screams rang out in the hallway, accompanied by repeated slapping sounds. I thought back to how Sam and I were pretending to be professional wrestlers earlier, and I thought that was what my mom was doing to my dad. I wondered why Sam was afraid.

The screaming got progressively louder as we listened. I could hear my dad yelling angry words and my mom crying. About three seconds later, the door flung open, missing my head by about an inch. I looked at Sam, who stared as if a tidal wave were approaching.

Watching that movie in the seventh grade, I came to the realization that my mother, who died when I was five, wasn't pretending to be a professional wrestler. She was getting raped and beaten . . . by my dad.

I sat on the couch next to all of my close friends with a lump in my throat the size of a baseball. The scene continued to drag out as many things became clear to me. I'd heard all of those noises before, but once the sounds were put into context, they made me puke in my own eleven-year-old brain. I still have the aftertaste.

The trouble with having a family is that you know every last sick and fucking twisted detail about them. There are no secrets. I have knowledge of so many things that I wish I didn't, and now you do, too. Sorry.

I spent most of my childhood hiding in the bathroom; that night at Zach's was no different. Sitting on his couch, I thought about my mother and I tried not to cry, but it's hard at that age.

After a few more visits to the bathroom, the other kids started making jokes. They thought I was jerking off in there. It is almost impossible for a group of junior-high boys to go twenty minutes without someone accusing someone else of masturbating, let alone when one of the gang turns the shit house into Walden Pond. The irony was that we were all doing it while frantically accusing everyone else around us of the forbidden acts we were committing. We were like young politicians.

While I had been in the bathroom, a small coalition had formed behind my back. On my fifth visit to the bathroom, they made their move. I could hear the insults and chants of my name even through the bathroom door.

My last visit to the bathroom had proven to them, beyond a reasonable doubt, that I was in there shocking the monkey. I was innocent, though. I wanted to set the record straight, but there was no way to explain the things that were going on in my head. No one could understand the trauma I was experiencing. I needed a place to hide from the sounds of my dead mother's screams, and the bathroom was my only sanctuary.

I came storming out of the bathroom in a rage, the biggest and angriest kid in the room. I wanted to take a swing at the nearest person, but I was outnumbered, and these were my friends. They were all I had, except they had me: masturbating, in the conservatory, with the lead pipe. Or so they thought.

I got so boiling mad that I stormed out of Zach's house. To this day, I am remembered as the kid who bolted out of a seventh-grade sleepover because he needed to jerk off really badly.

I continued walking down the street I grew up on, heading toward the main event. I did everything I could to avoid stepping on the cracks in the sidewalk. I never understood why people are afraid of the cracks in the sidewalk. It's just the way it is.

Despite the fact that my mind had just taken a vacation, I realized I was getting better at going about my business while I strolled down memory lane.

Philadelphia is all about "the business." It doesn't matter if you're going about your business, minding your own business, or saying something such as, "That guy's a prick. He does bad business." Doing business is the heart of Philadelphia.

But I kept forgetting that I was in Camden. I got scared for a moment that if I thought about Philly for too long, the youngsters around here would jump me. Things had gotten that bad.

I took the long way to my father's house so I could approach from the opposite side of the street. I hoped he wouldn't see me coming.

Seeing the building I was raised in opened the floodgates to the memories of the old neighborhood.

I was raised in one of those bi-level, cluster-fuck houses that had multiple families stacked up in it like produce at a fruit stand. The house would function like an apartment building in the sense that you had no privacy or water pressure, but it was still a house in the structural sense, and I found myself standing right in front of it.

In the summertime there was no air conditioning for anybody. The local crack heads made damn sure they stole as many of the window trophies as they could. Stealing someone's air conditioner right out of their window takes balls. Many of their attempts at theft were halted by fist-shaking tenants, but the crackies always win in the end because they never stop trying. The American worker is still the best in the world.

Every neighborhood is a tiny universe, and in my neighborhood, the planets orbited so close to each other that they almost touched. Every house had a porch, and the porch became a statement of identity, an expression of inner beauty, if you will.

The neighborhood had its token junkies, their front doors resting on broken hinges and their porches packed to the rafters with the useless crap they hoped to sell, one glorious day in the future.

There were the weirdoes, such as my dad and me, who never showed our faces, our expressionless porches blank and dusty as the seasons passed.

Every neighborhood has one of those ultrapatriotic veterans with more American flags than you can shake a stick at, and we had ours.

Last but not least, we had the Sanchezes, with their jungle display of flower power. Some people took the art of porch decorating to superhuman levels, and Juan's mom was one of them. No one ever took her plants because you couldn't really trade them for drugs or sex. The plants, which smelled good in the summertime, were like her little peace offering to the evil gods of the crippling environment that she lived in every day.

I glanced briefly at their house. From where I was standing, I could see the plants lying dormant in the cold winter. A daily newspaper, rustling slightly in the stiff breeze, lay on their porch.

Thinking back to my childhood made me realize that I was currently involved in a grown-up version of an Easter egg hunt. Except instead of hunting for a happy, pink egg, I was stealing back a loaded, forty-five-caliber handgun from the man who raised me. I missed the old days.

CHAPTER 2

CLOCKED IN THE FACE

reaking into a house is never easy, especially when it's the house you were raised in.

Looking around, I observed the colors of the predawn, bleeding into daytime. It would have been great scenery if I were walking out of a nightclub and high on drugs, but I was standing at the base of a staircase, looking blankly at the porch from my childhood.

Fearing the consequences, I turned to leave, but then I stopped, realizing that this had to happen. My gun was inside that house, and I needed it back. I began gently climbing the outside steps. They were old, and every step I took created a symphony of creaks and squeaks. Luckily my dad lived on the lowest floor, so I didn't have far to go.

I stood on the porch, toe-to-toe with my enemy, the front door. We faced each other like two evenly matched boxers, but I was hiding brass knuckles. The devious fighter smiled as he knew this would be easy after all.

Growing up, my trademark was to get the keys to most of the places I stole things from. The easiest way to break in to a house is to walk right through an open door. Keys are easy to steal then copy before the person even knows they are missing. My dad never noticed when his were gone.

One day, about two years ago, I went over to the house to find him passed out cold on the couch. The keys were on the coffee table. An hour later I returned from the hardware store with fresh copies of the house keys. I woke him up as though I had just arrived.

The stolen and copied keys had been sitting for years in a kitchen drawer as if they were fine silverware waiting for the guests to arrive.

My heart rate increased rapidly as I slid the never-used key into the door; the virgin metal was slippery smooth, making it hard to handle. The pounding of my heart was so loud that it reverberated all the way up to my skull like a stereo pumping out a heavy bass track. My nose hurt where I had hit it on the bus earlier.

Although I already had a key to get inside, I still hesitated because I wasn't supposed to be here. I had stolen a few car stereos when I was younger, and I knew the trick: breathe calmly; move calmly; and most important, stay calm.

Despite my strong résumé, the situation in front of me was different from anything I had ever seen. It's much easier to break into a car in the parking lot at the mall than it is to break into the house where you grew up. The car doesn't usually come with twenty-four years of baggage attached to it.

I glanced around to make sure no one was watching me while I loitered with cold feet on my own front porch. This was an odd situation.

When I had spoken to my father on the phone the day before, the tone of his voice scared the shit out of me. I had never heard him sound that weak in my entire life.

My gun had ended up in the middle of all this, and I was certain it would be resting snugly in my father's underwear drawer. When a man needs to hide something, whether it's a pornographic movie or a stolen handgun, stashing it in his underwear drawer is the most common approach. Perhaps it's because that's the last place another man wants to snoop around. I couldn't think of anything that would suck more than sneaking into my dad's house and rummaging around in his collection of outdated briefs. I also knew that if anyone in the city could do this, it would be me.

After taking three deep breaths of cold, winter air, I mustered up the courage to slip the key into the door. The creaking of the hinges sounded like the theme song to a haunted house as the door swung open.

At that moment it occurred to me that my dad, that motherfucker, had a key to get into my apartment the same way I had one to get into his. After all, that's how he got the gun in the first place.

According to my dad, Ron Sanchez wanted to kill him over a newspaper. It wasn't much information to go on, so I assumed that Pops had stolen my gun for protection in case anyone came looking for him. The smart bet was that Dad was running low on money, so he started stealing Ron's morning newspaper off his porch when he could no longer afford his own. Nothing is more infuriating to a man than interrupting the flow of his morning paper. My dad must have been pretty pissed off when his paper stopped showing up, and that's how Ron must have felt when he met with a similar fate. The difference was that Ron was still paying for his.

My dad had a reason to actually fear Ron would follow through on a threat. The crazy gangster with gold teeth had been calling for his head around the neighborhood. The word got around that some white guy was stealing Ron's newspaper every day off his porch, and I guess the symbolism of the whole thing was more than the neighborhood youngsters could stand. The important thing to remember was that Big Ron was one of the most respected people on the block. He was the oldest thug around, and he had done more time than anyone. It was a horrible résumé for scoring a desk job but a great one for scoring an ounce of coke.

But the truth at home is always uglier than the myth on the street. Behind the scenes, Ron Sanchez was physically abusive with his family. He beat his wife, whom he forced to raise his beat-up kids while he was constantly in and out of jail. I saw it all. None of this mattered to anyone in the neighborhood because Ron had respect, a rare commodity in our part of town. He owned a low-riding gangster bicycle that he would ride slowly around the block, proudly displaying his jailhouse tattoos like a war veteran in a parade.

The neighborhood showed the first signs of morning life. The old folks woke up and brewed tea. I heard a car door slam, followed by a second car door slamming a moment later. I needed to take care of business quickly, before the teenagers were awake.

The youngsters in the neighborhood were at the age of coming into their own. They looked up to Ron, and this was a dangerous situation. I was worried they would kill my dad over the newspapers. People who committed pointless acts of violence earned themselves increasingly greater reputations. In other words, acting like an asshole got you treated like a king.

The more I thought about it, the more I realized the bragging rights my dad's head would be worth around the block. The kids had a point to prove, and my dad was that point.

It occurred to me that there might be a second reason for Dad to steal my gun. Pops knew that if anything went down, the blame could possibly come back to me, not him. We both knew this; the plumber told us.

The plumber was a slack-jawed, overweight guy who talked our ears off when he came over one day to fix our toilet. I don't think my dad realized he was paying the guy the entire time he was talking, but the plumber rambled on, telling us stories about anything and everything.

One of the many and mundane topics the plumber spoke about involved his nephew's drunk driving arrest. Random, I know. According to the plumber, the public defenders in Philadelphia are so overworked that the only help they can offer most defendants is to assist in a plea bargain. The plumber said his nephew got screwed and you would have a better time sodomizing yourself with a tire iron than working with a public defender. Those were his exact words.

The plumber was full of stories that changed my life, like the one about the pressure point on every bottle of Heinz ketchup. Every diner in America stocks the same bottles of Heinz ketchup, and the bottle always gets clogged in the same spot. The ketchup backs up like traffic at rush hour. I hate it when that happens. The wise repairman told me that every one of those ketchup bottles has the number 57 embossed on the side, which acts as the pressure point for the bottle. All you need to do is thump your wrist on the sweet spot, and the ketchup is set free in a downpour of flavor.

A few days later, I was at my regular diner and the ketchup clogged. I pounded on the bottle, right where he told me, as I held it upside down. The dam broke effortlessly, and the ketchup came flowing out, while my steak knife remained clean. The important thing I took away from that experience was the plumber told the truth.

Dad knew that if he took my gun, registered in my name, and he used it to commit a crime, the law might come knocking on my door before his. He also knew the truth about public defenders.

Father knows best. He knew what might happen to me because he listened to the plumber, and so did I. On top of that, he knew that I knew that he knew it, and that put a little more ketchup on the wound.

I took my shoes off in the doorway and made my entrance, sliding down the hall in my socks as though I were ice skating. The familiar smells of dirty socks and cigarettes caused me to gag. I took a moment to reexamine the paintings I saw every day growing up. The generic pictures of sunsets and sailboats looked different through my grown-up eyes. I would never decorate a house this way.

I continued sliding down the hall in my socks, but the Ice Capades ended as I grudgingly arrived at my dad's bedroom door, which was cracked open about five inches. Standing at the entrance of his bedroom, I could feel alternating rushes of fear and adrenaline as I surveyed the scene.

Dad slumbered in bed, looking like a sack of potatoes. Dirty laundry was scattered all over the bed, while used plates and mugs littered the floor.

While I was watching him sleep, I realized I shouldn't be doing this; I was in the middle of doing a bad thing. The smell in the room was almost unbearable. I shuddered to think about the underwear drawer. Without giving it much thought, I held my breath and stepped across the threshold. I was in.

The task at hand wasn't quite as difficult as it might seem; my dad could've slept through an earthquake. Sleep takes on the form of a near-death experience when you drink as much grain alcohol as he did. Even so, I was scared that he would leap up at any moment and attack me, snores notwithstanding.

I inched across the room toward the underwear drawer until I heard his snores stop. My heart shot up to my throat in a geyser of bile. He was waking up.

I started mentally preparing my last will and testament, but then he dramatically went into a reprise of the melody of peaceful slumber. He was back to sleep. Game on.

I stood there, shaking, for a moment. After four more steps, I arrived at the treasure chest, his underwear drawer. I almost fell over in relief. The small, wooden box that housed the briefs hung partially open, with tighty-whities bulging out of it like snowdrifts. I regained my focus and opened the magic drawer the rest of the way.

With my back turned to the bed, I finally felt that familiar, relaxed feeling when the wheels of crime begin turning. Taking a deep breath, I thought about everything and everyone else in the city. I doubted that any of them were doing what I was doing at 8:17 in the morning.

I started leafing through the pile of underwear while I did my best not to think about it. Despite the bruise on my nose and the erupting volcano in my gut, I was taking care of business and getting the job done. Soon my rummaging hand unearthed the hidden metal treasure. The cold steel felt like pay dirt, whatever that is.

Picking up the gun, I carefully examined it in the morning light coming through the window. The gun looked different, but I knew in an instant it was mine. My hand fit perfectly around the grip, and I did what every little kid does when he holds a gun; I pointed it at the nearest person and pretended to shoot while making *pow* noises under my breath. I set it down on the dresser and did a little end-zone jig and thought about what it must be like to win the Super Bowl.

After dancing for a moment in silence, I realized it would require just as much skill to exit the house as it did to enter. The Holy Grail was back in my possession, but my business here was only half done. Leaving is always a bitch.

The rhythm of my dad's snores told me that soon the beast would arise and the morning ritual would begin. I collected myself and dashed out of the bedroom. I paused again in the bedroom doorway. My exit was amazingly smooth, almost too smooth.

The smug feeling of victory cascaded down my body from head to toe. I celebrated in the safety of the hallway. There's nothing like accomplishing the things you think you can't; that feeling of victory is hard to come by. I caught my breath and relaxed. Then a wave of fear buckled my knees.

It was then I knew that I'd fucked up, big-time.

Grabbing desperately at my empty pocket, I realized that I had forgotten my gun all the way across the room, on the top of the dresser where I found it. My throat clenched as I turned and spotted the gun on the other side of the sleeping giant.

A few seconds earlier, I felt like a man who had just won the Super Bowl, but now I felt like one of the Bad News Bears. I kept wondering how the fuck this could have happened, but much like Ron's gold teeth and my father's stolen keys, I would have to dwell on those important issues on the long bus ride home.

Right now there was no time to spare. My instincts told me to abandon the mission, go back to the drawing board, but I couldn't do that. I thought about leaving my dad's home as a failure. That fate seemed worse than anything I could imagine. Abandoning the mission was not an option. I prepared myself for the worst. With breath held, I let adrenaline take over and slipped out of my own body. To put it another way, I was in the zone.

The second time I walked into the bedroom was the opposite of the first; getting caught almost didn't matter at that point. Sauntering casually to the other side of his bedroom, I grabbed the gun off the dresser like a man taking milk out of the refrigerator. Then I stumbled quickly and loudly back into the hallway without looking back.

I thought about how it would require just as much effort to exit the house as it did to enter. Once again, I enjoyed the sweet taste of victory, in the form of cold steel in my hands, but I knew better than to celebrate around here. I had learned my lesson.

Although I hadn't bothered to be quiet when I went back into the bedroom, I realized how stupid that had been. I got lucky; the old man didn't wake when I tromped past his bed, but I had no intention of tempting fate. I'd heard too many stories about thieves getting caught making noise on the way out, once they got what they needed. A successful job is defined solely by your not getting caught at the end of it all. With this kind of lifestyle, the job is never done. I kept reminding myself of that.

I slid cautiously on my socks down the hall. From where I was standing, I could see both the kitchen and the living room. Both of the rooms had the eerie feel of an abandoned dollhouse. The house looked completely different. My dad definitely was not a good housekeeper. Picturing it without the crap lying around, I was surprised. The madhouse I grew up in was exactly like any other house I had partied in or stolen from. I wondered how it could look so normal, and it occurred to me, very painfully, that things could have been different.

I had been a nervous teenager, and I spent a lot of time by myself in the bathroom. I'll spare you the details, but the bathroom was the only place I felt safe, and it became my second home, in a sense. If bathroom Olympics were a sport, I would be the hometown hero of Philadelphia, but some things you can't brag about.

Anyway, there comes a point in adolescence when every young man starts obsessing about members of the opposite sex and pornography. Any man who tells you otherwise is lying. Let me tell you, whether you like it or not, porn is as much a part of this country as baseball, apple pie, and driving while intoxicated. If there were any issue that would ever unite this country, both Republicans and Democrats, it's that a man has the right to check out some tit in privacy when he's in the bathroom.

My thoughts drifted to this one afternoon—

Bam! My reverie was interrupted by the noise, then the pain, then the nothingness. Seconds later, my eyes opened to a layer of dust on the floor. Fingers of pain were sharply caressing the base of my skull, but all I could think about was how the floor needed sweeping. Dust was flying everywhere; there must have been an eighth of an inch.

As I was coming back into consciousness, I remembered what was happening. Damn.

I saw the fuzzy outline of my father towering over me. His appearance made the fear of god shoot through my veins like righteous lightning. The image may have been blurry, but I recognized that this was the same perspective of him I had when I was a little kid. Standing over me, he looked much taller than his actual height, like in a poster for a movie.

It occurred to me that while I had been reminiscing about my stellar masturbating career in the bathroom, he must have sneaked up on me.

Motherfucker, I thought, but then the pain in my brain dominated my inner dialogue, leaving me speechless, even in my own head. I lay there on my back, completely at his mercy.

"You ungrateful . . ." His tirade was loud but not terribly coherent. He was angrier than the words. His speech became mumbled as he struggled to think of more obscene obscenities. Finally a statement materialized.

"I'm gonna fucking kill you." When in doubt, turn to the classics. As I regained my inner voice, I thought about how predictable it was for him to say that. He could've come up with something better than that.

He straightened his fisted arm and connected it with my upper lip.

I blacked out for a second, and the comedian in my brain ran out of jokes.

Dad's words continued to echo in my head as I regained consciousness. This was getting old.

"You like that?" he said, though it was obvious I did not. "Who the fuck do you think you are, sneaking in here and . . ."

I tried to reply, muttering through my freshly busted lip, but that only angered him. I wondered why he was asking questions if he wouldn't wait for the answers.

"I need that gun!" His scream was so loud that my face shook from the reverberation. Fear pumped through my entire body once again.

"I got these fucking gutter punks . . ." He punched me again before he finished the sentence, and I couldn't understand the rest of what he said. My nose hurt so bad, it felt as if it had no skin on it. I thought back to when I accidentally hit it on the bus earlier; this time it meant something.

Words could not do justice to the pain I felt. I pictured two well-dressed people politely eating breakfast somewhere else. At this table, revenge was being served up, cold and proper.

My entire body went limp as I wondered if this would be the end for the main character in the story of my life. Meanwhile, Dad kept yelling about the bodily harms he would cause.

"You know what I'm gonna do?" he said through clenched teeth. "I'm gonna drag your sorry ass out to the shed and we're gonna have a little chat. Just like old times, you ungrateful little son of a bitch."

He had beaten me up in the storage shed before. I knew this wouldn't be good. Anytime he walked me out to a satellite location, it meant that I would get the beating of the year because none of the neighbors could hear. The shed also had a bunch of foreign objects he could hit me with. It was my family's version of a pay-per-view, no-holds-barred, steel-cage death match.

Over the years it had almost become a cliché for him to start hitting me in the house then walk me out to the shed to finish the job.

My dad was going to fuck me up, but this time I refused to allow it.

The downfall for a lot of these old-timers is that they have to make a Hollywood production out of every last punch they throw. Kids today are swinging like bananas.

My dad might as well have put up a billboard on the freeway, telling me that punches would soon be thrown. I pictured the advertisement, featuring his grinning marketed face as he held two thumbs up. The quotation on the ad would read, *In a minute or two, I'm gonna break a broomstick over your head. So if you want to do anything, do it now!*

I started faking an attempt to mumble some words at my dad. I knew he wouldn't understand me, but I needed to stall for a moment. Every time I attempted to speak, he put his face right up to mine and yelled louder as a means to silence me. He had one less bloody lip, providing him with an unfair advantage in a shouting match.

I learned at an early age that if you're going to throw a punch, do it first and do it on a low budget. Dad definitely got to me first, but now it was my turn to lie back and give him rope enough to hang himself.

He wanted this to be like a scene from a mafia movie where the boss threw his weight around. The problem for him was that while he was sitting on his ass watching gangster movies, I'd found a much happier home on the wrong side of the tracks, with people who weren't actors. My life wasn't a movie; I had been in and out of fights over one thing or another for as long as I could remember, and I knew those bullshit Hollywood scripts read a little differently on the street.

"What?" he shouted as he leaned in. I muttered a few more sounds while he looked at me with an annoyed expression, as if I were speaking a foreign language and he was doing his best to understand me.

I mumbled again.

"Jesus H. Christ!" he screamed. "Why don't you just say you're sorry. You . . ." He continued with his sermon of guilt, but my nomadic mind had a religion all its own. His words made me remember that I wasn't the kind of person who worshipped an abuser. Then I remembered something else.

There's a place on a person's forehead with no pain nerves. It's three inches above the part of the nose I hit earlier on the bus. Most people don't know this. Back when I was in high-school gym class, the teacher showed us how to slam our faces into a soccer ball without knocking ourselves out, though one girl did anyway. I listened attentively on the day he taught that lesson to the class, but I had a completely different agenda than the rest of the children.

As I struggled to breathe and cowered on the ground underneath my dad, I remembered that I knew how to turn my skull into a sledgehammer of destruction. Even though my arms were pinned, I could still fight back. I looked deep into his eyes. The time was right; I made my move.

Bam!

The crack of my head on his was as loud as anything I had ever heard, and I didn't feel a thing. Contact had been made; this was good. During the collision, I had heard the sweet sounds of popping blood vessels harmonizing with bones cracking onto bones. The noise sounds like victory because if you're the one awake enough to hear it, it means you're winning.

It was odd but after I had flung my face into his skull, I found myself wondering if I had done a bad thing. Then a series of childhood flashbacks, happening in an instant, nailed the coffin down.

I remembered the time when I was a little kid and I got my ass kicked by my dad because I stretched out the neck of my T-shirt.

Then I remembered the first time, several years later, when I figured out that the T-shirt he beat me up over was a lot cheaper than the bottles of whiskey he drank all the time. As a child, I saw a lot of whiskey bottles getting thrown into the garbage, but not that many new T-shirts.

When I was nine years old, my friend Rick Clark invited me to go swimming. I ran into him at the community baseball park one day, and the next thing I knew, I was in the back seat of his mom's car, heading for the action.

In my excitement to go swimming, I had left my bike, the one Dad had stolen for my birthday, at the park, unattended. I was young. I had gotten distracted because for one of the few times in my life, I got to be a normal kid playing with other normal kids. When the sun began setting at the pool, I remembered my bike, clear on the other side of town.

I left the pool without saying a word and ran all the way back to the baseball field as fast as I could. When I arrived, the park was dark and my bike was gone. I'd never felt so alone.

Upon arriving back at my house, my dad questioned me as to the whereabouts of the bike. I thought back to the day he had stolen it, and tried explaining to him how we were all playing a big game of tag, and now it was my turn to be "it," but the irony of the joke was lost on him, and I was met with angry hands.

As the collision of cartilage slowly became a painful reality, my dad whimpered and fell off of me, slumping on one arm. He went silent and still a moment later; I must have knocked him out.

I sat up and surveyed the scene once more.

Dad looked like a corpse, stretched out in the wife-beater and boxers that passed for pajamas. My instincts told me to sit him up straight and make sure he was all right. I had just cleaned his clock, but I was afraid to touch him. The only way to go was out.

Standing up and looking around in disbelief, I observed the area of the hallway we had just fought in. It looked like a tornado had torn right through it. I wondered if he would ask me to fix all of the broken things a few days later. That would be awkward.

Without warning, Dad rolled over onto his stomach; it scared the crap out of me. For the life of me, I couldn't understand why I was still afraid of him. I was standing tall on my feet, and he was lying there like a bum in the street. It occurred to me that I could have spent my entire morning kicking the crap out of him. I had scores to settle and more issues than *Time* magazine. I had never fought back against him in my entire life; the head butt had broken years of silence.

I realized this would be the perfect time for a classic, family-style beating that you would see in a mafia movie. I could see the movie promo in my head: A young man returning home for payback, plus interest. But for some reason, I wasn't enjoying any of this.

My life was not a movie.

I was hungry and I wanted to spend the rest of this fucked-up morning putting my hands all over an egg-and-cheese sandwich, not some smelly, old man.

It was at that moment I realized I had the option of leaving. I was never much good at rising above violence, but there comes a point in some situations where forces you don't understand take over.

Turning my back and walking through the miniature kitchen toward the door, I thought for the first time in my life that I had actually done some growing up. Leaving home felt like the right thing to do.

While I was reaching for my shoes and congratulating myself, I realized once again that I didn't have my gun. He had taken it from me during the beating.

I cursed as loudly as I could, jumping up and down in a fit of rage. I wondered how the fuck this could keep happening to me. After retracing my once-righteous path through the kitchen, I stared stoically at the aftermath in the hallway.

Dad was still visibly shaken, but he was up on all fours. The gun was resting a few feet away from him, lying there like a jellyfish in the sand.

I was amazed at how he'd gotten the gun out of my pocket during the fight. I found myself respecting his tenacity; he was a real American. The longer I stood there, though, the more the respect gave way to the familiar panic and fear.

Holding my breath, I plunged into the hallway. Keeping my distance, I picked up the gun carefully, like a doctor removing an organ during a surgery. Exhaling the breath I had been holding, I turned to leave. The whole thing seemed easy as pie. I should've known better.

As I was strutting away, Pops swiped my feet and tripped me up.

Like a fool once more, I slammed face-first into the wall, dropped the gun, and landed on the floor.

Pops regained his composure. Remaining on all fours, he lifted his head, surveying the scene. Seeing the gun on the other side of me, he stretched for my torso.

Like father, like son. I reached for the gun. The moment was priceless.

He clawed his way back on top of me. At that moment, the truth became clear to both of us. If Dad got the gun first, it would be a double whammy for him; he would get to own the gun and kick my ass, but if I got the gun first, it would be a hat trick for me: the gun, the ass-kicking, and a hot breakfast would all be mine.

We fought like two children. The scuffle resembled a game of Hungry Hungry Hippos, our hands competing earnestly for the hot potato. Sadly no matter which hippo got to the gun first, he wouldn't really win all that much.

His forearm found its way to my throat, putting him back in charge. I knew a fist to my face would soon follow. I realized this was a fight I wouldn't win, but then I realized something else.

Ethics are important but ethics take on a completely new meaning when you're physically fighting with the man who raised you over a stolen handgun at 8:28 in the morning in the house you grew up in.

He spit in my face, and I knew what I had to do.

I kicked him in the balls.

"You bastard!" my father screamed. "You . . ." He struggled to talk, but the pain had become unbearable.

As soon as he fell off me, I sprang to my feet and put my gun in my pocket, where it would remain for the rest of the day.

He coughed in pain, and his face pressed against the dusty wooden floor. I looked at his shirt, stained from the dirt on the floor, and wondered who would be the one to clean it. He looked up at me with a disappointment that was unparalleled.

"You're supposed to mmrraagghh . . ." He choked on his words for a moment, until he found his voice and stuttered. "You're s-supposed to s-stick up for m-me, and you come here and k-kick me in the balls? You b-bastard! They're going to kill me, and you don't even care."

I had never been so shocked in my entire life. My actions made sense to me, but the concept of family responsibility was another story.

I knew deep down that I was supposed to stay here and stick up for my dad when trouble came knocking because that's what children do for their parents. The family unit is the building block of society, and here I was, kicking my dad in the balls when I should have been defending the homeland to the death.

My shame was awesome, but then the facts of the situation came back into light, and my reasoning stood on its own. He asked me a question, and for me the only answer in sight was the door. These issues would have to be sorted out on the bus ride from Camden to Philadelphia. In the meantime, Dad had raised another topic that I needed to address.

"Ron's not going to kill you, Dad." I spoke in my adult voice, doing my best to handle the negotiations. "The situation is simple. If you leave his newspaper alone, they will leave you alone."

Earlier in the morning, I had noticed that Ron's newspaper was still on his porch, where it belonged. I took this as a good sign, like a peace offering from my dad to Ron. In a neighborhood as bad as this one, talk is cheap and attention is short. The majority of these kids who make threats don't back up every last thing they say; if they did, they'd be pretty busy.

The kids on the block cared a lot about Ron's paper, but they didn't care that much about my dad. Like most people, Dad was guilty of thinking he mattered more than he really did.

I would never be able to explain it, but in the middle of all this, I did have underlying concerns about Dad's well-being. It was instinct. Deep down, I knew that I would never permanently turn my back on my despicable family obligations, unconventional as they may be. Despite everything that had happened in my life, there was something inside of me that wouldn't have let this situation go south, not today and not tomorrow. Although I had never admitted this to myself until he raised the issue a minute ago, I knew that I should be sticking up for my family, horrible as he was.

My ghetto intuition also told me that this was the last scene in the newspaper opera; the fat lady had sung. The two parties involved here could sink or swim on their own, without my gun or a group of aspiring gangsters in the mix. My mission here was complete.

Even though it wouldn't happen for a while, I also knew that I would return home at some point. Family is inescapable. That's why it sucks beating them up. You're only beating up yourself.

As I headed out the door, I heard my father walk toward me and say something, but I wasn't interested. I went about my business.

Holding my sneakers in my hand, I walked down the stairs. Once I got to the bottom of the staircase, I put my shoes on. The sidewalk was an unusual place to lace up a pair of sneakers, but living with the greatest cheap-shot artist in history will put you in odd situations.

While tying my shoes, I could feel the winter sun hitting my back. The concrete underneath me was beginning to thaw, and so was I. It felt good to be outside with the colors.

Maybe it was just the pattern of the morning, but the smell of Old Spice rattled my cage. I was a fool to think I could relax around here.

After finishing the second double knot and raising my head, I could see big Ron Sanchez standing directly in front of me, larger than life and very pissed off.

As I straightened up to look at him, I could see that he came to fight. He was wearing his favorite running suit, which was not good. Normally a person wears their least-favorite clothes when they know there will be a scuffle, but with Ron, the opposite was true. I knew that this was his big day, his moment to shine in front of the whole choir. Big Ron was planning on fighting, winning, and maybe even getting arrested in front of the neighborhood kids. He needed to look good when he showed the youngsters how he handled things, and if he got arrested, then so be it. He truly didn't give a fuck.

He was staring at me. I stared back.

Looking at him in the context of the previous twenty minutes, he seemed a lot smaller and fatter than I remembered him. Gray hairs were showing themselves like the first blades of dead grass in the fall. He had developed crow's feet from squinting while he stared excessively at strangers, and his once-beefy neck had assumed a jiggly texture as old age had its way with him.

As our eyes met, a silent but defiant exchange unfolded on the sidewalk. My posture shifted forward. I realized there was no hell on earth that could compare with what I had just been through.

Don't get me wrong; Ron would have pounded my pumpkin all morning, right in front of my own house, but fighting is about more than boxing. Ron recognized the look in my eye. It was as if he could see my entire morning, my entire life even, reflecting in my bloodshot eyes.

Ron knew how to kick my ass a million times over, but he was caught off guard by my sudden homecoming. He wasn't the only one. Ron slowly realized that if he planned on beating me up, he would have to kill me to do it. There was absolutely nothing he could do to me that would make my life any worse.

I thought about his son Juan, and my eyes filled with rage.

A fight is nothing more than a poker game of hate. Whoever holds the most hate usually wins the fight. Bluffing is everything. Ron might have had the upper hand with his many decades on the street, but he could not understand the stack of chips in my eye.

He stood five feet away from me, like an urban cowboy, forcing a look of anger that displayed his gold teeth. Ron was upset about a few mornings' worth of newspapers, while I had just fought off a lifetime of abuse.

He kept staring at me in that way I hated. He could see the filth from the fight all over my clothes and the fire still lingering in my eyes. For a moment, his gaze assumed one of warriorlike respect. We had both come to fight the same enemy. We were both burning with the same rage.

Ron understood the hate that was consuming me that morning; it had consumed his whole life. Although in reality, Ron was a wimp. He only acted tough toward people who were smaller and younger than he, such as his wife and kids. That had never occurred to any of us because we never stood up to him.

After a while Ron realized he wasn't looking for a fair fight; he had come to push an old man around. He didn't have the stones to spill his own blood this early and this sober. Once a level of mutual respect had been reached, I broke our stare and glanced at his newspaper, still on his porch, almost instructing him to go home.

My defiance presented a problem for Ron. He needed to leave on top, but he was going to have to fold.

He broke into a fake laugh as a way to show he won the standoff. He pointed at my dirty clothes and my damaged face. His eyes went to my head, just under my hat. I reached up and felt my hair sticking out. I tucked it back in as fast as I could. They can never see my hair.

Ron swiped his hand in a dismissive motion, implying that he wouldn't get involved. The gesture implied that he felt Dad and I were doing a fine enough job of killing one another.

He turned and walked back to his house, his mission complete. Just as on that day in the bathroom with Juan, no words were spoken.

I walked away.

Five blocks away from my dad's house, the sun had risen high enough to shine on my side of the street. The warm air felt good on my split lip, but it didn't last.

Anyone who lives in the same neighborhood for long enough can tell time without a watch by studying the position of the sun on the buildings. After looking at the sun, I knew what time it was; it was time to go.

I was walking fast enough to build up a bit of a sweat. The dampness on my shirt and my pants reminded me that I had left this morning with wet clothes. I couldn't stop thinking about the situation with the change machine. I had the money, but I couldn't finish drying my clothes because the machine was out of quarters. It was aggravating.

I didn't understand the point of opening a business that doesn't do business. A change machine is supposed to provide change. I could understand if the machine ran out of quarters once in a while, but considering how often people came up to me begging for change, it must be out all the time. How the fuck is anyone supposed to clean clothes with no quarters in the machine?

The more I walked with a wet crotch, the more aggravated I got. Every step I took reminded me of the fact that someone failed at doing his job. It's wrong to tease people with laundry machines; all they want is to clean their clothes and go about their day. There should have been at least one or two days when the machine had quarters.

I pictured the fat guy from the Monopoly box, laughing and watching me on video monitors the entire time.

Bam! Suddenly the people on the street around me stopped what they were doing and stared at me.

I looked around in confusion. When I realized my hand was hurting, I knew what had happened. I had gotten so upset in the middle of my mental tirade that I had punched the speed limit sign on the street as hard as I could. Pedestrians within earshot had turned to look at me as if I were some lunatic.

In my head I cursed the owner of the Laundromat, whoever he was, and continued down the street. I struggled to think of something, anything that would help me calm down.

I had come upon a group of homeless guys, standing around a shopping cart and listening to music. The seasoned street dwellers had a boom box in the top part of the shopping cart.

I stopped walking and listened for a moment.

Biz Markie is a cool dude. After listening to that guy for thirty seconds, it's hard to feel bad about anything. His hip-hop was blaring out of the boom box, and the gang was singing along, out of tune, with the Biz, who was also singing out of tune.

I like the song where the Biz keeps repeating the line, "Damn, it feels good to see people up on it."

My friend Zach started throwing real parties, where he would DJ, as soon as we got in to high school. One night he had a party and kept throwing that vocal sample into the mix. The tiny living-room nightclub was packed with girls, and the vibe was jumping. I stood there, grinning. A fat joint had just circulated around the room. I looked over at preadolescent Juan, who was smiling as wide as his mouth would stretch. It did feel good to see people up on it.

Growing up, there weren't a whole lot of good times to speak of, but we made them count.

Looking around at the assembly of homeless people and shopping carts stationed next to one another, I could see that some of them were huddled around the cover art from the album, studying it intently. The plastic wrapper from the compact disc lay discarded on the ground, the price tag still on it.

I thought it was strange for a group of homeless people to go to a store and buy a Biz Markie album when they probably needed money for food. Nobody pays for music anymore. Even the kids in the college dorms are copying everything illegally, breaking the outdated copyright laws and opening the floodgates of free music.

After a minute it occurred to me that the homeless guys didn't pay for their party music, either; they shoplifted it from the store. The difference between the bums on the street and the kids in the dorms is that the bums steal things the old-fashioned way, with balls.

As I moved a little closer to the music, I could hear the Biz's voice faintly. He was doing a cover of the song "Benny and the Jets" by Elton John. When the Biz kept saying, "Benny! Benny!" the crowd went wild. The homeless guys sang along, and it sounded great. I wanted a copy.

The excitement around the packaging changed because one man was hogging the glossy paper. The rest of the people complained as the capitalist sat with perfect posture next to his shopping cart. He examined the cover art quizzically, wearing his best intellectual expression.

The old man looked up from the album cover and stared at a beautiful woman walking down the street. Her blonde hair bounced as she walked, and her sexy business suit showed under a khaki trench coat.

She was showing only about eight inches of her stockinged leg, but apparently this was cause for excitement. Not even Biz Markie could compete with a hot piece of tail.

"Oh, yeah! That's some leg, baby!" the homeless man shouted out with a misplaced Cajun accent.

I didn't think the legs were very exciting.

The walking woman looked directly at me as soon as the words rolled off the bum's tongue. The winter goddess he was heckling thought that I had made those comments.

"In your dreams." She looked me up and down. I still had dirt and blood from the fistfight with my dad all over my clothes. My lip bled slowly. She wasn't impressed. "Loser."

The crew of bums celebrated and laughed hysterically when they realized I was getting blamed for something they did.

I stepped away from my newfound friends. I got the impression they didn't like me. I was the wrong color.

The woman strutted confidently through the intersection toward the hospital, where she probably worked at some high-paying job. There's nothing in Camden for a girl like her except for that hospital.

I thought about running alongside the woman and charmingly explaining to her that it was the homeless guys who yelled out those mean things, but I knew it wouldn't make a difference as she went about her business.

Life is hard when you come from a broken home. It's like being a jockey in a horserace where your horse never makes it out of the starting gate. You end up sitting there the entire time, watching the other horses going places while you just get farther and farther behind.

Across the street, I could see a woman closing her bedroom window with a disgusted look on her face. She didn't like what I hadn't said, either.

I looked at my watch. It was 8:42 in the morning.

CHAPTER 3

THE DEBT

After a couple of weeks, John and I couldn't take it anymore. We had to get Ralph.

Decent members of society have an understanding that certain behavior is unacceptable, while others need to have things explained to them.

We had no choice. We had to kick his ass.

John and I boarded a city bus in the early-morning freeze. By that point in the year, the strangle hold of winter was slowly beginning to loosen, but it was still pretty fucking cold.

The beating from my dad was now a few weeks behind me. During that time, I had been able to do a good job of hiding my beat-up face while it regenerated, but I did an even better job of hiding Roberto's money while that regenerated as well.

Roberto was my drug dealer, an older Mexican guy who spent several years in prison and didn't take no for an answer. For years, we had been stuck in the revolving door of debts and bad habits, but we always managed to honestly keep track of who owed what to whom. People say that trust is going out of style, but few of them realize that without it, the black market doesn't exist.

Over the past year, I allowed myself to feel slightly comfortable with Roberto. I knew I was making money for him the entire time, but our association put dinner on my table and a roof over my head. I appreciated that. Life isn't always black and white. Bad people do good things sometimes, and I often wondered where I would be without Roberto.

My strategy was simple: I would take out a loan to cover a debt then worry about the loan later. I made Brad pay for his weed up front, many hours before he would receive anything. It was an unusual arrangement, but he trusted me, and on top of that, he didn't know anyone else. I would take Brad's money and give it to Roberto. Then I would "borrow" the weed from Roberto that I had already "sold" to Brad.

It sounded confusing but our situation was a lot like musical chairs at that point, and I sometimes wondered if we could just add a chair. For example, if I decided to forgive Ralph's debt, then Roberto could forgive my debt, and Ralph could look the other way when someone stuck him on money. But that's not how musical chairs works. When the music stopped, we all had to sit down, and the ugly truth was that we were short one chair.

The heart of the beef with Ralph was the money he owed me over a football game that had already been played. The score was final, and the consequences were set. There was no turning back for any of us, but for some reason I kept wondering about the logic of what we were doing to one another. We were spilling real blood over simple math. It seemed a little dorky. I felt like one of the nerds from the dorms who take their fantasy football league way too seriously. The debt between us was over nothing more than numbers on a sports page, and the idea of our being slaves to a system that we created ourselves seemed absurd.

I thought back to when Ralph's apartment was robbed six months ago. He didn't have much stuff, but they took it all anyway, and I'd heard of his struggling ever since. After I thought about it, I realized practically all the people I knew either owed money to others or had money owed to them. I kept going back to the idea that if we all looked the other way, just one time, it would be like pressing the reset button on a video game, and we could all get on with our lives from there. But the longer I thought about it, the more I knew in my gut that it was bullshit, complete bullshit. Blood had to spill or else the game wasn't real. It's a sad fact, but any time a team of professional athletes takes the field, it guarantees that bones will break in the real world.

The conclusion I reached was that in a world based on speculation, the buck stops on the same point where the bullshit ends. For me that point was on Roberto's couch at the beginning of Emeril's show, the moment I needed to have cash in hand.

It sounds cool when you spell it out like that, but that was twenty-six minutes ago, and now I was just sitting on the bus, bored. I hate it when the person sitting next to me treats me as though I'm part of the armrest.

John had just spent the past twenty minutes doing so, and it was a complete invasion of space. The bus is public, and so is the armrest.

"I had no idea the ride was going to take so long," I said to no one in particular.

"Bitchin' about it ain't gonna help none," John snapped at me with his eyes still closed. My normally sharp right-hand man had been reduced to mush. Tequila. I had seen him like this before.

There's something I need to explain. My friend John is actually Juan Sanchez, the kid from across the street my dad told me I wasn't supposed to play with.

Roberto is Juan's uncle.

When Juan was in the fourth grade, a substitute teacher couldn't understand how to pronounce his name. The teacher got flustered, and after an awkward pause, he called out the name "John Sanchez." Young Juan tried to explain things to the teacher, but the teacher took his comments as a "yes," and class moved along. Juan Sanchez became John Sanchez for the day. This country is like bleach; we whiten everything.

"Help any. It's not going to help any," I corrected smugly.

I often forgot we weren't the same race. Don't get me wrong; racism was all around us every second of the day, but making money was the only thing that mattered to the two of us.

When old people look at the world today, they see nothing but a bunch of colors, but when the younger kids look at the world today, they see nothing but a bunch of numbers. I think it's a generational thing.

John sat in awe of the process of thinking. Twenty seconds later he had forgotten that anything was said. "What's not going to help?" he asked out of the blue.

I shook my head in disgust, and ten seconds later, he was back to sleep.

It was a rare morning moment. John was still drunk from the night before, and his sharp wit had been reduced to incoherent babble.

I looked out the window and wondered if we were up to the mission at hand. We didn't even know where to find Ralph. We had an idea where he was, but we weren't sure.

Becky, our regular waitress at our regular diner, told us she had spotted him working at the Happy Burger across town, but that was a while ago. We weren't sure Ralph still worked there or if it might be his day off. We were rolling the dice by spending an entire day on this.

I leaned forward in my seat and rubbed my eyes, realizing I still had sleep funk in the corners of both of them. I tried rubbing it off on my pants, where it didn't blend in. It appeared as if I had blown my nose all over my lap. I could tell this wasn't going to be my day.

Television sucks. They got the whole thing wrong. If this were a television show, John and I would be sitting in a brand-new car, listening to some hot rap single while we made stern faces and cruised through vintage Philadelphia scenery. But this was real life, and instead I found myself slightly imprisoned on a city bus route through the slums. It felt like riding a carousel around the inside of a toilet. People don't pay attention to failure; this isn't the main part of town.

I took a moment to watch a hooker on the street as she tore through her purse, looking for something. She was standing adjacent to a liquor store with a broken sign. Somebody had stolen the *T* off the sign above the store so it read simply *Liquor S ore*. This is the greatest city in the world, but on a clear day, the slums surrounding it looked like a living graveyard. The drunk, broke locals staggered around like zombies, as if they were already dead but the bus was late to take them to heaven.

Some aspects of urban life are so indigestible that Hollywood can't even begin to address them in prime time, such as the pile of brown, rotting diapers in someone's front yard or the fact that the hooker had begun digging through her crotch with the same intensity she used looking through her purse. No network would touch this shit with a ten-foot marketing pole.

John was the one with the hangover, but his breath stank so badly that I was the one feeling nauseated. Every time I inhaled, I could smell the combination of grain alcohol and a kid who hadn't showered last night off himself.

The bus was crowded. We couldn't sit in the back, so we had to sit close to the driver. That bothered me. I liked to sit in the back. During the ride my underwear started creeping up my thigh; then it slowly and painfully pinched my left testicle into my leg. I liked to wear the white briefs just in case the cops ever search me, so I had dealt with the tightening testicle vice before. I knew the only way to solve the problem completely was to stand up in the middle of the bus and slide my hand all the way down my pants to readjust my ball sack. After performing that dirty deed, I would have to retuck every layer I was wearing into my crotch while everyone looked at me. That's not something that people do, but I stood up in front of a captive audience and did it anyway.

"What are you doing?" John asked, looking up at me in a daze.

"Scratching my back," I replied.

"From your crotch," John said sarcastically as he sprang to life. "You just sent your hands on a fishing expedition in your freaking trousers, right in front of my face. And now you're telling me the real problem is with your back. And the area next to your dick that you've just been scratching like a turntable, that's your back as well?"

I was up on my feet, looking down on him as he looked up at me flatly. The moment was more than I could handle. Standing tall on my feet, I made an announcement to the bus in a loud, drunken, Southern voice.

"The back o' my ass, y'all! Uh-huh!" I sang to John, but everyone else attended the concert as well.

Did I mention the bus was packed?

I squirmed, feeling the judgmental eyes of everyone on the bus gazing at me. I thought about how things looked from their perspective. If you were one of the people sitting behind me, then the only thing you would have seen was me jumping to my feet and diving furiously into my crotch, where I spent over a minute fondling myself before I sang about my ass.

My reality show runs every day of the year without flashy commercial breaks or much of a plot line. The writer must be on vacation or something because this shit is all a waste of time. That writer's a dick.

Less than a minute later, my stomach growled as my mind wandered. I was hungry and I couldn't stop thinking about how badly I wanted a sandwich. The hunger pangs made me remember one lunch that I had with Ralph several years ago. We had been friends for a while. It surprised me that he stabbed me in the back the way he did.

The legendary lunch occurred a few years back.

Around that time, a chain of sandwich stores was opening all around Philadelphia. These stores were different because they were the first to serve the sandwiches piping hot with cheese melted all over them. Every time I stopped by Ralph's place, one of their commercials was on his television, and the announcer was boasting about his toasted lunch. Lots of fast-food places serve hot sandwiches now, but back then none of them did, and poor Ralph and I were forced to eat cold sandwiches every day. The idea of a submarine sandwich baked up like a pizza was like the invention of the wheel in our eyes. We would watch the commercial with our jaws on the ground, visions of melted cheese resting snugly on Black Forest ham graced his dusty television screen. We talked about it a lot, and we decided we would go to the grand opening together.

When the big day finally arrived, we smoked a record amount of weed before noon. Then we made the seven-block pilgrimage to the store, which was like walking fourteen blocks for Ralph because he was nearly twice my size.

When we arrived at the store, I could see that the party balloons and streamers were all hanging in their proper places, but things weren't lining up the way they were supposed to. The inside of the store was dark, and a middle-aged guy with a mustache standing out front was apologizing and telling people the grand opening would be tomorrow. He started explaining something to us, but Ralph called him a fucking asshole, and we walked away. Strike one.

The next day I decided to pick up the sandwiches on my way over to Ralph's because I felt sorry for him. I was always feeling sorry for him. That's probably why I shouldn't have loaned him money in the first place.

For as long as I could remember, Ralph had a passionate hatred of onions. They made him gag, and they pissed him off. I never realized what an onion-based society we live in until I started dining heavily with Ralph. The funny thing was, he never told the waitress to hold the onions. The only way he knew how to express himself was to freak out on the poor girl when the food arrived. Funny stuff. Americans love their onions, but I've noticed they don't find unattractive people with complicated lunch orders to be quite as lovable.

So it was no surprise that they showed me no mercy at the sandwich shop. I even asked them to hold the onions several times, but when I arrived at Ralph's apartment with the brand-new sandwiches, I discovered that I got onions, like it or not.

Strike two. This pissed me off. Springing to my feet, I told Ralph that I would take care of this immediately. Customer service was not dead. That's what I told myself as I hustled his sandwich back to the store then back to his apartment yet another time.

Upon returning, I bragged to Ralph about how I told the people at the store to hold the onions five times, just to be sure.

Ralph had been losing money hand over fist that month. I just wanted the kid to have a fucking sandwich so he wouldn't be so grumpy when he forked over the dough that he owed me.

I watched with pride as Ralph bit madly into the sandwich.

He had been waiting on it a long time. Ralph looked like a stray dog tearing into a steak, except stray dogs don't spit their food out all over themselves once they've tasted it. He coughed and fumbled for his soda.

I knew what was going on. I had seen this before.

Onions.

This greatly pissed Ralph off. He ran to the sink and gargled out every last piece of onion with the soda that came with the meal. In between the angry gargling noises, he squeezed in colorful profanity and punched the sink in a rhythmic manner.

I wished I'd had a tape recorder.

Without a word, Ralph furiously grabbed every bit of food and packaging that I had brought into the house and bolted out the door. He almost ran headfirst into his cousin, who arrived along with his girlfriend and his roommate.

I had met them all once before, and I didn't like any of them.

Although Ralph's cousin had come over to talk to him, Ralph had urgent sandwich business at hand, and he was gone with the wind, leaving me alone with a bunch of fucking randoms.

We passed the time with standard small talk, and I hated every minute of it. I didn't appreciate that Ralph had left me alone with people I barely knew, but my time would soon be well spent.

Twenty-five minutes later, Ralph returned with a half-eaten cold sandwich from the corner deli and a pale expression on his face. I knew instantly that things had gone wrong at the sandwich shop, but I had no idea just how wrong.

"I shouldn't have done that," Ralph said remorsefully. He sat on the couch in a stoned daze.

"Done what?" I asked excitedly. I knew that some shit had gone down, and I was dying to hear about it, but Ralph's cousin's girlfriend started nagging about how their group needed to get going. They'd been waiting a while, and she had been complaining the whole time. I was upset that she interrupted. The more time Ralph had before telling his story, the better able he would be to change his story to lessen the full impact. I knew that some shit had gone down, and I needed the straight scoop.

"Dude, what happened? Tell me everything that happened. Right now." I repeated my need for the lowdown.

"I just—I shouldn't have done that," Ralph said quietly.

After several minutes of prodding Ralph while blatantly ignoring the girl, Ralph dished. It turned out that by the time he walked all the way to the store, he had a few things on his mind.

"As soon as I got in there, I went right up to the register, and I threw the sandwich down on the counter. Then I took each piece of bread and slammed it down on the counter while I yelled out the phrase, 'I said no onions!' at the top of my voice. After that, I got so mad that I rubbed each piece of bread around on the counter, making as much of a mess as I could. The sandwich was cut in half, so there was four pieces of bread, one for each word."

I wished I had been there. Ralph was really finding his groove.

"On my way out of the store, I delivered an individual 'fuck you' to every single customer and employee in the store, women and children included. Then I walked outside."

Strike three. Ralph was out.

I knew every word of his story was true except for the part about him walking out. It was obvious that he ran for his life because he had big armpit

stains and it wasn't even hot outside. He must have been afraid the employees at the store were going to call the cops on him, so he had to haul
ass on the way home. He was sitting on his couch with a blank face and a
half-eaten Wonder Bread sandwich that he had purchased from a store that
sold mostly liquor and beer.

There wasn't anything more I could do to help him out. I had shit to do
all day. I had to take his money and run.

"It was that same fucking asshole with the mustache from yesterday."
Ralph slightly choked back tears of anger. This wasn't that funny for him.
"That guy couldn't do his job to save his life."

Suddenly my face became as blank as Ralph's. "Wait a minute. That guy
from yesterday?"

"That same one. It was that same dick-head from yesterday," he said.

He was as clueless as I was speechless. There was dead silence in the
room.

Ralph's cousin and his crew had been sitting on the couch, watching the
entire conversation like a tennis match, and now things were about to take
an interesting turn.

"I really yelled at the girl working the back of the sandwich line. I let her
have it the most," Ralph continued.

During the time I had been waiting on Ralph at his apartment, I took
a moment to ponder the mysteries of sandwich creation. In the beginning,
the sandwich is ordered at the back of the line. Then it goes through the
oven before it comes out at the front, near the register and the onions. I had
placed my order with the person in the back, and they are powerless fig-
ureheads in the world of onions. I came to the revelation that the person at
the front of the line is the Big Daddy of onion distribution; they're the ones
you need to get nice with. I wished that I could have figured this out and
explained it to Ralph before he left.

"I screamed and screamed at the girl standing at the register," Ralph said. "I called her every name in the book."

I was laughing inside.

Ralph had exploded on the wrong sandwich-shoveling employee, but that was only the beginning of his mealtime misfortunes.

"You went to the wrong store, Ralph," I said flatly.

A golden silence filled the room, interrupted by only the sound of Ralph's cousin's girlfriend's gum chewing. Things had suddenly gotten very entertaining, and they were no longer in a hurry.

Looking around the room, I noticed I had a captive audience, so I continued. "I took the subway to get here today. I didn't stop in this neighborhood. They just opened another brand-new store right over by the subway station, on the same day as the other one. You went to the wrong store, you hollered at the wrong people, and now you're eating the wrong sandwich. That store we went to yesterday is like twenty blocks from the one I went to today." I paused and wondered if it were too late for Ralph. "Maybe you can still go back?" I asked him.

Ralph turned a deaf ear to what I was saying. He knew that he had soiled his reputation so poorly in the one store that word was sure to travel around the city then the world. Every local sandwich shop employee knows the legend of the Screaming Onion Monster of Northern Philadelphia, appearing out of nowhere at grand openings then vanishing into the abyss, never to be heard from again.

I shook my head and laughed. I hadn't thought about that story in a while, and I might have forgotten it if I weren't in this mess. It's important to remember the funny stuff, but it wasn't that funny for Ralph. Although, after I thought about it, I realized Ralph's life might not suck so badly if he learned to lighten up a little bit. After a couple of days, any fuck-up can be turned into a joke or funny story, just like that slapstick sandwich scene. Essentially that's what all our lives in Philadelphia were, a long, rambling joke waiting for someone to tell it in just the right way.

During the time I had spent revisiting our previous lunchtime follies, we had arrived in Ralph's neighborhood. John and I stepped onto the street and spotted him through the Happy Burger window, working behind the counter, just as Becky said. The target was within sight. We ducked into an alley before he saw us.

Drugs. Man, I loved weed. After we had taken cover on the side of the restaurant, John unexpectedly found half a joint that he had forgotten about from the night before. We crouched in between two dumpsters and enjoyed the breakfast of champions.

I coughed into the cold city air as the familiar taste of burnt rope filled my mouth. Suddenly I was a lot less annoyed, and I cracked a half smile as I pictured Ralph sweating on the couch that day. Smoking that joint felt like putting a bandage on my life, and somehow all of this bullshit felt natural, as though this were the way everything was supposed to be. I knew there were much better places I could be at lunchtime on a Tuesday—when you're poor, they never let you forget it—but after that smoke-out session, it seemed there was nowhere else on Earth I belonged. Crouching down and looking around at the alley, I knew I was home.

Everyone has a purpose on this planet, and mine was to occupy that alley right then. A debt was owed, and the reason for my existence on this planet was to collect it. Getting stoned in that alley, I realized that when life gives you lemons, do drugs. I liked getting high. Everybody has an internal voice that never shuts up. When you're walking down the street, the voice tells you that you're hungry and you need to eat pizza; then the voice starts mindlessly reciting the numbers on license plates and so on and so on. The voice never stops; it's maddening. When I toke up, there is absolute silence in my brain. I liked it when people were quiet.

I don't do any drugs except weed. I've tried a few other things here and there, but there's nothing like the chronic, and tens of millions of tax-paying Americans would agree with me.

A few years back, I tried rolling with the whole ecstasy thing, but it wasn't my style. I would go to those all-night parties, and I would get paid all right, but I got tired of babysitting a bunch of dumb shits with pacifiers who came from good homes. When you're hanging out at those parties and your pockets are full of that crap, you become a magnet for these wandering gangs of clueless zombies who won't go to bed. It's like a bad horror movie: They follow you around from club to club. They show up at your house for breakfast at eight in the morning. They never go away. The whole freaking country is searching for salvation on a Sunday morning. I'm not trying to be anybody's Jesus.

It sounds cool when you spell it out like that, but that was fourteen minutes ago, and ever since then, I had been leaning up against the wall while precious silence rang out in my smoked head.

But we lived in Philly. Quiet doesn't last.

Out of nowhere, I felt a burning need to holler at a red-headed woman I saw walking down the sidewalk on the other side of the street. The sexy red-head was more than I could stand. I hate red-heads so much that I had fallen in love with her, and I had to express my tender feelings to my new sweetheart.

"Hey, baby!" I screamed in the girl's direction. Then I physically moved John to the side so I could get better acoustics. I continued blaring, "Hey, sweetheart! You know my eyes aren't the only thing that's blue!" I paused for effect. "My balls are, too!"

The pretty pedestrian turned around and scoffed in disgust. She was a complete stranger to me, and I was a complete ass to her; it was a modern romance waiting to happen.

"I tell you, these red-heads are the scum of the earth. Scum of the earth," I repeated to John.

"Wow." John was so flabbergasted by my previous statement that he could barely talk. He was speechless and I was proud.

The performance needed a closer, and I had one last jingle to do the job. I yelled again in the red-head's direction, "Hey, sweetheart! Since I fell for you, I got a song in my heart and a stink in my fart! Let's have a mocha sometime!" I shouted the phrases louder than anyone had ever shouted anything. Then I made the "call me" sign with my right hand.

John cringed with every word.

My new girlfriend stopped walking and gave me the finger before she walked down the street and out of my heart. The gesture showed me she was willing to go that extra step for our relationship, and I knew I was in love. One of these days, one of those girls would walk right up to me and violently break my nose and jaw. Then I would laugh.

I leaned back and continued talking as though nothing had happened. "Do you feel like hearing a joke?" I asked nonchalantly.

"Sure," John said in a disinterested voice.

"This was a joke I wanted to tell to that hot chick Brie when I saw her at the cookie table the other day."

"I could go for a cookie right now."

"Me too," I agreed. Unfortunately the cookies were back at the college. "So I seen them talking about the cookies that day, and I had this joke I wanted to tell them. It would've been the perfect joke to tell to those girls right then and there, to get my foot in the door with those sorority girls. I don't know any of that crew, and this joke would've been perfect."

John had that "get to the fucking point" look on his face. Anyone who's ever performed on a stage or even read a book report in class has seen that look, and it's not good.

"Here it is," I said dramatically before pausing to take a breath. My timing was every bit as perfect as my delivery. Honest. "I like it when people say, 'I'm dropping the kids off at the pool,' anytime they have to go to the bathroom." I took a quick pause for effect. "I can't wait until I'm a dad and I have a van full of my own children that I'm dropping off at a local swimming pool. I'm going to roll down my window and yell to the other parents, 'I'm taking a shit!'"

"That's good," John said. He tried to hold back laughter, but he failed miserably. "That's good," he repeated in a more sincere tone.

The sight of someone laughing at my joke got me pumped. Everyone has a dream they fall back on when they're stuck in traffic, or they're trying not to blow up at somebody. We all want something better than what is in front of us. I want to be a comedian. I want to be on *Saturday Night Live*. I doubt that I'm funny enough, but being a wiseass is the only skill I have. The only thing I know is that my life sucks, and at least that's a foot in the door.

"How perfect would that joke have been to tell those girls?" I asked John while punching his arm rhythmically.

Back when I was a kid, one of the few times I saw my mom and dad laughing together was when we sat together and watched John Belushi on *Saturday Night Live*. I always remember the way my parents would smile when his show was on because it didn't happen very often.

Several years later, when I was a teenager, I remember wondering what John Belushi was doing, but then I found out he was dead. It sucks when a funny person dies . . . a lot more than when a nonfunny person dies. Comedians help make the world a better place, and when they're gone, the world is a shittier place because of it.

His death got me thinking. Good comedians can make anything look funny when they're on a stage, but off stage, there's not much to laugh at. All the best comedians seem to have the same suicidal tendencies, as if every one of them were haunted by the same personal demon. After a few jokes, they find something in the laughter that makes the demon go away, just for a minute. Then the jokes become an addiction.

When you laugh for the first few seconds of a joke, you're just like anyone else in life. You're going places and you're on the team, just like those people catching a free ride on the subway. The joke almost becomes a place to hang out for a minute or two, like a big soup kitchen serving up the status quo. Day after day, you end up getting dependent on the one thing in life that makes everything all right. You would do anything to get it back, even steal an air conditioner out of someone's window if you had to.

The one thing I learned watching John Belushi is that you'd better have some serious problems if you want to keep people laughing after the first couple of years. Over the course of my life, I had developed an acute sense of how to tell a joke because I had to; it was the only way I would survive. Comedy became the equivalent of a baseball bat that I would use to kick the crap out of any problem that made my life hell. Let's just say that the bigger the problem, the bigger the bat.

"I tell you, though, Manny, I don't know if those girls would've liked that joke. Those girls are in the most exclusive sorority on campus." He paused. "I hate to break it to you, but that joke is one that you tell to homeless people and other stoned clowns like you and me, guys who stand around in alleys, smoking pocket roaches while they're waiting to stomp the crap out of some lowlife."

"No, it's not. Everyone will laugh at that joke."

"No, they won't."

"Bullshit," I insisted. "If you saw somebody tell that joke on *Saturday Night Live*, you would laugh your ass off. And so would the rest of the country. That joke is funny. End of story."

"Manny, this ain't *Saturday Night Live*. You're a fucking screwup. You're a goon telling a dirty joke to a better-looking goon. Nothing more, nothing less."

"Half of that may be true, but consider the fact that my joke is funnier than anything you would see on television, even if you watched all day."

"That's why I don't watch television," John said in a sly tone. He knew he was winning the argument. "People in Hollywood don't have real problems; they don't crack real jokes."

"Those girls would've liked that joke," I said arrogantly and leaned back against the wall, but the more my buzz began to wear off, the more reality set in, and the more I realized that I wasn't getting any younger or better looking.

"Ralph," John said bluntly.

Right, Ralph. Suddenly I remembered why we were in the alley in the first place; then I remembered that John had slept on the bus ride over, so we had arrived at Ralph's workplace with neither strategy nor game plan. This was probably the time to think one up.

I stared at the brick wall opposite me as if I could see Ralph working on the other side of it, only a few feet away. He was unaware of the many harsh realities of gambling. I think he viewed life as a big game of golf, and he thought everyone else would adjust their scores because of his many handicaps, but that wasn't the case.

"So how's this gonna work?" I asked John.

It was a pointless question because I already knew how it would work: we were going to kick Ralph's ass. But the situation in front of us was different from the others, and lately I had begun questioning our methods.

John laughed. "Are you joking? What do you mean by that? You mean to say, 'Where's this gonna work out?'" He straightened up. "Ralph's gonna get his, and then we're gonna get ours." John's delivery was enough to convince me at first, but my empty wallet told another story.

I gave him an incredulous look.

John's face twitched with rage. "Well, what the fuck else are we gonna do?" He knew I was questioning time-honored traditions, which society frowns on. Fuck society.

I decided to answer his question with a question. "Where's Davey Zapelli?"

This confused him even further. "Why the fuck are you bringing up Davey Zapelli, and why the fuck would you think that I would know where he is? If I knew where the David was, do you think I'd be wasting my time on some small-time punk like Ralph?" He tried brushing off the subject. "I don't know where that asshole is. I think he's in Florida right now."

CHAPTER 4

THE DAVID

Davey Zapelli, better known around our neighborhood as the David, had some impressive talents, including mooching, not shaving, and an unprecedented ability to heckle women in broken English. I had never seen anything like it. All the neighborhood girls knew and hated Davey. He was a standard-issue East Coast Italian kid: loud, proud, and not allowed in bars more than once. High-school weightlifting had turned him into a brick of a man, a block V-8 engine that ran on booze and smokes, but time and alcoholism had made him as soft as a sofa on Sunday. As the years passed and the hormones dwindled, his body began to resemble a vacated industrial park, an obnoxiously oversized and unsightly monument of better days long gone.

Zapelli had a shady side. He was associated with a high-rolling drug dealer from Pittsburgh. The guy would come into Philly every couple of weeks for a coke deal that paid Zapelli's bills several times over. Aside from that, the David didn't want to know shit. He smoked and drank every night until the sun came up, and every day he ate in the same diner at the same counter. He owned an expensive leather jacket, and his reputation was that he treated the jacket better than any of the women he'd dated. One of the David's trademarks was trying to explain himself using big words that he didn't understand, but ultimately he was unexplainable. Zapelli was an enormous clown and a great friend.

One night around Christmas about two years ago, on the way home from one of those Pittsburgh deals, Zapelli was feeling saucy and decided to stop off at his regular strip club. His associate wasn't expecting the product until the morning, so Zapelli decided to spread a little yuletide cheer at the club, the way he always did. The smart move would've been for him to drop off the brick of cocaine before he went out and got drunk at some butt-crack shack, but when it came to brains, Zapelli was a few sandwiches short of a picnic. At the end of the night, the David learned that someone else liked his leather jacket even more than he did. The jacket and the product were gone, and Zapelli's life in Philly would never be the same.

Zapelli made only a small cut off the Pittsburgh deal; the mountain of blow in the jacket belonged to his associate. The David was forced to repay a sum of money he simply did not have, so we didn't see him for months. When the jacket disappeared, so did Zapelli.

To complicate things even further, when Zapelli left town, he also walked out on a nine-hundred-dollar gambling debt owed to John. Zapelli had placed the bet before his jacket got stolen, when he was still in good standing with everybody. The day after the big man's boner at the strip club, his team lost the big game and John was stuck holding the bag.

In the months that followed, we heard reports of the David being spotted in the area around Rutgers University in New Brunswick, New Jersey. After a lot of begging and a lot of free pot, we convinced one of his many sisters to set us up with his whereabouts.

John and I promised her we wouldn't tell the David who gave him up. We also told her we would never to do anything to hurt a homey from the block. Honest.

The Friday after we got his whereabouts, we spent the entire afternoon on the fucking bus on our way down to Brunswick. I owed John a favor, so I told him I would roll with him and watch his back. The buses ran late, the trip took hours longer than we thought, and as usual we didn't discuss a strategy or plan of attack on the ride over. We arrived late and pissed off. After stopping off at a diner for a quick plate of pancakes, we found ourselves positioned on the magic block right in front of all the bars. It was almost midnight.

Rutgers is no different from any other college in America. The kids flock to neon signs like moths to a flame. When it came to locating Zapelli, all we needed to find was a crowd and a couple of Budweiser signs. A blind man could have found Zapelli at Rutgers.

The moment John and I first saw his face in the crowd was something I will never forget. The David was drunk, staggering up to a stranger to bum a smoke.

When he first saw us, he looked flustered, then embarrassed and sad, but as we finally approached one another, I noticed he was forcing a look of pleasant surprise onto his guilty mug. We had seen the complete range of drunken emotions on his red and embarrassed face in less than thirty seconds. Priceless.

An unlit cigarette dangled from Zapelli's mouth as he opened his arms slightly and shrugged. People on the East Coast use that gesture to express two things: "I got love" and "What's up with you? Where you at?" Zapelli wanted sympathy from us, and as far as he knew, we had plenty of that.

In a surprise move, John mirrored Zapelli's open-armed gesture. The exchange morphed into a friendly hug, and the two of them looked like estranged relatives reuniting at the airport.

I stood off to the side with a look of confusion plastered all over my face.

Zapelli looked about ready to cry a tear of joy as his emotional range came around full circle. In his wasted state, he kept returning to one popular catch phrase: "I gots monies for you guys. I shwear it," he slurred. He turned to me and explained further. "It not alls that I owe, but I gots money right now. I so sorry." The David had been drinking heavier than on the average night, and his broken English was more broken than usual.

It appeared that the moment had gotten to John. A plate of pancakes can do a lot for a man. John's stomach was full, and his heart had changed, or so it appeared. "Look, I heard about what happened," John said in an understanding tone.

I was shocked.

"I so, so, so sorry."

"We still need to even up on this. This isn't over," John said politely and without emotion.

I finally understood the point John was trying to make. It wasn't about the money, although that was important. It was about respect and the simple fact that members of society should be held accountable for their actions. Forget about good deeds and good manners. Violence and intimidation are the glue that holds society together. In a peaceful world, nobody gets paid.

"I know, man. I know. I want to repay the monies."

Based on John's unusually relaxed posture, it appeared that our journey to New Jersey was more about making the David apologize than anything else. The David now had the option of making good on his mistake, and he seemed eager to do so.

"I be a dead man in Philly. I knows it." His eyes pleaded with us. "But I working down here. Gots my motivation on, and I wants to make good. I swear it." Zapelli was probably expecting a response as full of drunken emotion as his was, but John and I were two thugs who ate one too many pancakes. Our demeanor remained flat and unresponsive.

"We smoke," he declared and held out a joint to show us that he was serious about providing the things we desired. "My boy Sonny gets this weed down here. I mean this shit is *platonic!*"

John and I both nodded then casually walked away from all the lights, all the witnesses. Ninety seconds later it occurred to me that Zapelli used the word *platonic* instead of *chronic* to describe marijuana. Classic Zapelli.

The three of us strolled down the street together and joked around like old times. My blood was still boiling over Zapelli's leaving town the way he did, but something about seeing a familiar face and hearing a voice from back in the day changes things. I looked over at Zapelli as we walked, and I thought about his situation. He got robbed. It seemed to me that as long as he paid the money to John, we should let it go. He didn't leave town to run away from John; he left town because he owed $20,000 to some big-time gangster none of us knew. I glanced over at the David one last time as we entered the alley. Zapelli wasn't some deadbeat who ripped us off. The kid was family.

Suddenly the David yelled at a group of attractive women walking past us down the street. "Hey, baby!"

The girls were approaching the line of people waiting to get into the bar. After hearing Zapelli's outburst, they seemed to be reconsidering that place.

Zapelli turned to me and spoke under his breath in an official tone. "See, if you don't catch the eye contact with the hoochies, then it's just wasting everybody's time." He turned away and shouted across the street a second time, "Hey, baby!"

That caused the girls to turn around and face the David.

"Hey, baby! Don' worry about the long line!" He turned to me and smiled. "As long as I gots a face, you always gots a seat at the bar!"

That did it. They turned around and walked quickly in the other direction. Zapelli tried yelling an encore, but in his wasted state, he had let the fish wiggle off the hook.

However, the three of us had a bigger and greener fish to fry. We ducked into the alley.

The David laughed as he lit the joint and passed it to me. He had been cooped up at his sister's boyfriend's house while he on the lamb, and he told us stories about having to listen to his sister crying out in passion every night as her boyfriend fucked her brains loose.

I could tell Zapelli was rattled about seeing us unexpectedly, but in that alley, he was still as funny as he'd ever been. To me the true test of a comedian is being funny when life isn't, and Zapelli passed with flying colors. My breathing slowed as I relaxed my posture. This was going much differently than I imagined it would. I exhaled a huge cloud of smoke and thought about all the other circles of friends across the nation, sneaking out for a quick smoke on a Friday night. For thirty seconds, it was a snapshot of a normal life.

Bam! That's exactly what it sounded like, and I'll bet that's exactly how it felt.

Zapelli collapsed like a demolished building. The light but familiar breeze of a swinging arm blew through the crisp, evening air, disrupting the thick cloud of smoke. Stepping back from the circle, my buzz skyrocketed through my head like disco sales in the seventies.

I had been confused into thinking we were a normal group of friends, but nothing was farther from the truth.

In his drunken state, the David, who had just been writhing on the ground, began crawling toward the roach, which I had dropped when John hit him. The truth was indigestible, so the only thing Zapelli could understand was there was weed on the ground, and he wanted another hit. It never occurred to him that he had just been sucker punched by his good buddy John, and it was sad.

John grabbed my arm.

I knew this was bad, so bad that John didn't even have time to put it into words. Instead, he just put the squeeze on the nearest limb.

Red and blue lights illuminated the alley.

I knew what to do.

We ran toward a fence that separated the back of the alley from an abandoned warehouse yard. A cop car parked outside the alley where blood and weed had just been exposed. Maybe they saw us; maybe they smelled us; maybe they didn't. We didn't stick around.

Before I even realized what happened, I was forced to climb a fence—not one of my specialties.

A bright white searchlight appeared in the alley as we began scaling the fence. The light scanned around the corridor furiously, like a cat looking for a mouse.

I was not doing a good job of climbing the fence, slipping and falling repeatedly. Dangling from the steel wall, I couldn't stop wondering how we were going to get paid at the end of all this. Zapelli didn't actually give us any money, although he said he would, and now there was no way for us to continue a nonviolent dialogue with a kid who was bigger than both of us put together. As I tried again to get over the fence, I watched the last expensive cell phone I've ever owned fall out of my pocket and break into a million little pieces. Since that night, I've been so broke that I can afford only cheap cell phones with loud ring tones. It's hard to get laid with a phone like mine. I lost a nice phone and a good friend in that alley; I haven't seen either one since.

The other lesson forced on me that night was that sucker punching a man guarantees return payment in kind. Three months later I got thrown out of a nightclub for no reason, and the bouncers roughed me up in the alley. The big men talked shit to me the whole time. They were friends of Zapelli's, and they let me know it.

The cop lights trailed off in the distance as I finally reached the summit of the fence and crash-landed on the other side. John and I ran across the warehouse yard and into the obscurity of a Friday night on a college campus. As we headed back to the same spot where we had reunited with Zapelli earlier, it occurred to me that all had not been forgiven, far from it. In the middle of all the mixed signals, John and I had been able to get the point across that what Zapelli did was a bad thing, but now we weren't much better.

I laughed slightly under my breath as I thought about Zapelli yelling at those girls. He's the one who taught me how to heckle pretty women. I learned how to express myself from the master. Before that night in the alley, every time I yelled obscenities at girls on the street, I thought about the David and how he would handle it. Now all I think about is the David crawling back toward that roach, not even realizing he'd been duped. Don't get me wrong. I still yell shit at women all day long, but it's never been the same.

There's an odd rhythm to life when people steal. A stranger had stolen Zapelli's jacket at the strip club, forcing Zapelli to steal from John by not paying the money he owed to him. Then John had stolen Zapelli's trust by sucker punching him in the alley. When the bouncers Zapelli knew beat me up outside the bar, they stole my Friday night as payback for what John did. On top of all of that, fate had stolen my phone in the middle of the circus. I wondered about the person who stole Zapelli's jacket on that fateful night. That person was like the one domino at the front of the line that started the chain reaction.

John and I walked briskly down the Brunswick street, and it occurred to me that we would have to wait until tomorrow to return to Philadelphia. The buses didn't run at night, and Zapelli was the only person we knew at Rutgers. Sleeping on his couch was no longer an option. Despite the glaring idiocy of all our actions, one question reigned supreme over all the others.

"So why did you wait all that time to hit him?" I asked of John.

"I know. I was gonna do it right away, but he wanted to light a joint. I ain't dumb." There was new confidence in his stride.

We continued walking in a familiar silence that spoke volumes.

Finally John exploded. "Well, what the fuck was I supposed to do?" he yelled out.

I wanted to hit him.

"I didn't have to sucker punch him?" he asked me sarcastically. "That's bullshit! He's the one who sucker punched me! All these years of friendship I had with the David and he didn't even have the decency to call me and say, 'Hey, John, I'm about to rip you off and leave town.' Well, I'm sorry, M.C., but I didn't have the decency to call him and say, 'Hey, Zapelli, I'm about to punch you in the face.' He sucker punched me, so I sucker punched him back. Now we're even."

Ethics are like funhouse mirrors, they have an odd way of reflecting themselves.

"I would've thought that getting his money first would have been more logical. Maybe then we could stay in a hotel or take a late-night train." The sobering reality of where I was standing and what time it was slowly surrounded me like the stench from a bean fart. I felt like Ralph did that day on the couch; I had ended up with the wrong sandwich. "This shit ain't right." I looked around at the unfamiliar streets, wanting to go home.

"Hey, Manny, you park in the crosswalk, and you're gonna get stepped on!" Ah, John's famous catch phrase. He loved saying that when things didn't go his way. "Ain't my fault!" John shrugged and kept on walking, although we didn't know where we were going. As we continued along on our journey to nowhere, I could see the regret all over his body language. John knew he fucked up, but he got to deliver his catch phrase, and that was all that mattered to him.

Catch phrases suck because they allow a guy to live his life like a jerk-off, making senseless decisions as a means to lose money hand over fist, while appearing to have some kind of noble purpose. All was forgiven when it came to John and his slogan about the crosswalk. He was only returning the favor society had paid him. Tit-for-tat.

CHAPTER 5

KILLING TIME

The daydream ended but the issue remained.

"So what's your solution, genius?" John asked in an angry voice.

I hadn't said anything for a while; thinking about Zapelli brought back a lot of memories. However, the truth was I didn't have any idea what to do. It's easy to tell if a car is broken; knowing how to fix it is another story. I thought about the night we confronted Zapelli at Rutgers, and I knew there was a point I had to make, but no matter how hard I tried, I couldn't figure it out on the spot. Being a poker player, I decided to fill the silence with a lot of bullshit said in a confident tone. I knew the right cards were in the deck; I just needed time to shuffle.

"Check it out," I said while straightening up and acting as if I had a plan. The first thing I did was rehash the obvious. "We need to get paid. I need to get paid, or it's my ass this time. And if we're gonna get paid, we're gonna have to be patient with him, and we're gonna have to use our heads."

"You wanna head butt him?" John asked. "M.C., that's you're solution to everything. We're not fightin' your old man here."

"No, you fucking moron. I'm talking about using brains to get cash instead of using brawn to . . ." I had to stop talking since I couldn't finish my thought. I'm not really that smart. After a few moments, I gave up trying to think, and I just shouted, "You know what the fuck I'm talking about! If we beat up Ralph in his own neighborhood, the only thing that's gonna happen is he's gonna switch neighborhoods. We got lucky on this address. We just can't expect that Becky's always gonna be there to give us his next address. Becky would shit a brick if she knew she helped us out on this one, and she would shit a bigger brick if she saw us in person, in her neighborhood, stalking Ralph."

"True. But I don't give a fuck about Becky, and I don't give a fuck about Becky's opinion."

I was impressed. Becky was a pleasant waitress, and she liked our crew, but she was bipolar and had a mean streak like nobody's business. I used to joke about how I was glad she didn't work in a steakhouse or a gun factory.

"Fuck Becky," John concluded.

"Hear me out. If Ralph slips through our fingers again, then he's gone for good."

John nodded slightly in agreement.

I stood there with an expression worthy of a slightly successful safe-cracker. I knew there was a certain combination of sentences that would get me everything I needed, but that was all I knew. Then it hit me, or so I thought. "This is what we're gonna do. Remember when we were kids, and you used to play that game, sort of like tag, where you follow someone around for hours without touching them, and no matter how far they run, you never let them get more than an arm's length away?"

John shrugged then gave me a cockeyed glance.

"C'mon! Remember when we were little, and we used to tease kids by following them around for hours, like you were their shadow." I cracked a smile because I was talking out of my ass at that point. "I think that game's called Shadow or something like that." I started to laugh.

"I never played that game."

"Me neither. It doesn't exist. But that's how we're gonna get paid on this one. I know Ralph. I go back with him. We all do. He always fucks up, but he always comes around. No matter what kind of bullshit excuses he throws our way, I say all we do is follow him around, even if it takes all day, until he gets tired and goes back to his house. He'll want his Oreos. Then we follow him home, and then we have his address." I clapped my hands once for emphasis.

"He'll never show us where his house is."

"If we follow him around all day, he will. That's where his food is." True to form, I was beginning to believe my desperate bluff. One of the reasons I don't go to school is because I don't need to. I know how to play cards. I felt pride in the way I had just taken a bullshit hand and made it a winner. "Once we have his address, we give him a week. He'll need time to cook up that much bread. Next week, we show up at his house, and at that point, once he's thought about the fact that we're supposed to be his friends and he's thought about the fact that we're never going away, his ethics will make him beg from relatives and force him to finally take that long walk to the pawn shop. Look, he already knows that what he did was a bad thing."

"His ethics aren't shit, Manny. If he knows it's wrong to steal from his friends, then why did he do it?"

"Hey! You're the one with the fake textbooks in his backpack. Go see what Brie's analysis of the situation is because if you ask me, I'd rather be getting paid in cash instead of running around and acting like professional wrestlers in some misguided attempt at teaching a bunch of lowlifes the lessons that life was supposed to have taught them already."

We stared at each other.

I'd actually thought this part of the argument through on the bus. Ralph wasn't going to have the twelve hundred dollars he owed us in his pocket. This whole process was going to take a minute or two, but as long as John and I were present in Ralph's sphere of life, I knew he would slowly begin coughing up money. Violence meant consequences, like it or not, and on top of that, I'm just lazy. But that wasn't the way we did business in Philadelphia.

"What are you, Muhammad freakin' Gandhi or some shit!" John shouted. "Let's kick his fuckin' ass! Right here in this alley!" He motioned to the open area in between the two massive, green dumpsters. The eight-by-ten-foot area afforded us privacy from the street and only one entrance. It was a perfect location for a studio apartment . . . or a two-on-one ass-kicking.

"Asshole, it's broad daylight out here," I said with as much frustration as I could express. "I don't know what the fuck you're thinking on this one. Personally, I want to walk away from this without having to pay ten times what Ralph owes me back to the city, back to some scumbag lawyer." Yes, I had considered the possibility of our getting arrested while beating up Ralph and what that would cost; then I would be spending thousands just to lose hundreds. Life, and the city of Philadelphia, has a way of sticking it to me like that. "You dumb motherfucker, look at yourself. Your pockets are packed full of god-knows-what, and you're runnin' all over the city, wantin' to fistfight with people on the goddamn sidewalk. As far as today is concerned, you ain't gonna get nothin' out of him except his lunch money and a pair of sore knuckles. And it's *Mahatma* Gandhi! It's not Muhammad! Mahatma is a title; it's not a first name."

John scoffed.

I realized I had just won two arguments simultaneously. It wasn't a trifecta, but I was getting closer.

John continued staring at me in disbelief, and we spent a moment listening to the awkward silence.

"His apartment just got robbed; they cleaned the whole thing out," I said calmly. "He's gonna need a minute or two to get this together. We'll fuck him up when the time is right."

"His apartment got robbed a long time ago. That's no excuse! Manny, you're playing games that don't exist. Here in Philadelphia, we play tag. Tag!" He punched his hand. "Now he's it! When we're done with him, he's gonna look like O.J.'s wife, when she burned O.J.'s turkey, on O.J.'s Thanksgiving. That's how this is gonna get handled." You need to understand that right now. Ralph's whole life is nothing but a number on your books. He doesn't have thoughts, feelings, or any of that other crap that women get into. He's the thieving, little bitch who stole bread off of your table and nothing else. What are you gonna do if you ever have kids to feed, M.C.? Not for nothin', you're in the wrong line of work, homes."

"You've been saying that ever since high school," I said with a dismissive wave.

"And you've been getting burnt by these knuckleheads ever since high school!" John lowered his voice. "You're in the wrong line of work, thinking like that. Maybe you should go over to Roberto's and tell him the truth about your little money situation with Ralph, and you should go tell him about your emotional feelings for Ralph, and how Ralph's apartment got robbed. So what if Ralph has a shitty life? Boo freakin' hoo. Sounds like it's time for you to go back over to the dorms and push Brad around some more." John snickered.

I began to suspect that kicking Ralph's ass meant more to him than the money, but he was still hung over from the night before, so the argument was an easy sell.

"Maybe you should go online and download some friends," I said sarcastically. I had to cool things down. We were starting to fight with each other when Ralph was the enemy here. "Look, we're ignoring the eight-hundred-pound gorilla in the room."

A few months ago, I was watching the evening news and the anchorman made this metaphor about how everyone else in the newsroom was ignoring the obvious facts of the story they were covering that day. He said they were ignoring the eight-hundred-pound gorilla in the room. Since then, I've heard a couple of people talk about ignoring the eight-hundred-pound gorilla after they farted

John sniffed the air for a minute, wondering if I farted.

I wondered if he knew there was a legitimate use for that term. "The fact remains, at the end of all of this, we need to get paid. Cash money. Scaring him around from one neighborhood to the next doesn't fatten my wallet one bit. I'm not scared of Ralph, not one bit. I just think the fear of him getting an ass-kicking is just as effective as him actually getting his ass kicked. It's less risk, less work, and I'll be damned if I have to run around fighting like *Muhammad* Ali over some three-digit debt." I made sure to emphasize the name to indicate the proper place for it.

John stood there for a minute then nodded in agreement.

I continued with my new strategy for extraction. "We sit tight, right here, and then we wait for the moment when he comes down the street. Then we step out and begin having a friendly conversation with him."

John and I both had wanted to confront Ralph for a while, but we knew we would lose business to spend a whole day tied up with this nonsense. During the time we had spent waiting in the alley, I had already gotten several calls that could have proven lucrative. The situation made me angrier every minute, but too often friends had taken advantage of us and slipped through our hands. Not this time. We positioned ourselves about five or six feet deep in the alley, just far enough away from the sidewalk so Ralph wouldn't see us until it was too late. There is nothing as priceless as the moment when debtor and the one owed finally meet face-to-face.

I guess in the end, life isn't about who cares about whom or what's fair; life is about showing up on time and paying up on time. The lesson that I get out of all this is to pay your bills and shut the fuck up about your problems. End of story. That's what I do, and there was no reason Ralph couldn't do the same.

We were a lot alike. I pictured him running home from the sandwich shop that day. He couldn't control his stomach or his temper, and neither could I. In the end there wasn't much difference between us, except that I had a faster metabolism. Sometimes I miss the kid. Life sucks.

So John and I had a strategy, a plan of attack, and backup plans on top of the other plans. We were set.

Sobering up as best I could, I allowed my adrenaline to pump. I realized this was the moment we had been waiting for. Five phone calls, and 118 minutes later, I had grown so impatient that nothing could keep me in that alley one second longer. A disturbing thought occurred to me repeatedly, and I had a hunch I was onto something. After dwelling on it for about half an hour, I burst out of the alley and onto the sidewalk without warning. Our cover was blown.

I boldly walked down the street and right up to the window of the hamburger shop, looked inside, then returned to the bunker to face John's scolding about how we shouldn't let Ralph know that we're in his neighborhood, but none of it mattered. Ralph was gone and I knew what happened. As far as today was concerned, it was over.

Hours ago, when we first arrived on the block, we observed Ralph in the restaurant from across the street. It was lunchtime then, and the restaurant was packed, so he didn't see us. After the mealtime rush, only a skeleton crew worked the afternoon shift. When they no longer needed the extra hands, Ralph had gotten off work, walked out the front door of the Happy Burger, and turned left to go to his apartment. Unfortunately our alley was on the right. We hadn't considered that was an option, so we didn't get to eat.

John and I walked back to the bus station, feeling like two proud lions that had let their prey run off in the desert. I knew I'd failed at my job.

The next day, John and I took the bus back over to Ralph's neighborhood. Round two, more trouble. A favorite hobby of mine is eavesdropping on people in public. It's a lot like sitting in front of a slot machine: mostly a waste of time but every now and again it pays off and you feel like jumping up and down when it's all over. Today was my day.

When John and I had boarded the bus, we sat behind a middle-aged couple. The guy was stocky with a large mustache and well-combed hair; he looked friendly. The lady, who wore a ton of makeup, sparkled with fake jewelry. Anyone with that much real bling wouldn't be caught dead riding public transit.

I got bored talking to John sometime around the eighth grade, so I leaned forward and let the good times roll.

"So she comes home from school, and she's tryin' to tell me she's a vegetarian. Know what I'm sayin'?" She had a strong Philadelphia accent that is difficult to transcribe.

"A vegetarian?" the man said. "I'm a Sagittarius myself, born in December. What month is vegetarian?" His timing was flawless.

"No, silly," she said as she smacked him playfully. "She doesn't eat meat, you know what I mean? That's what a vegetarian is, know what I'm sayin'? Sagittarius is your . . . Oh, what the hell am I explaining this to you for?"

"'Cause you like to hear yourself yap." He sat back confidently. "'Member when we was kids in science class, and yous used to tie two coffee cans together with string so you could hear what the person on the other side was sayin'?"

"Yeah."

"For your birthday I'm gonna get you a pair of headphones like that. You'll have a can for each ear!" He laughed. I could tell he was his own biggest fan.

"Stop it," she said as she nudged him. "So she comes home yesterday . . ." She paused. "Wait a minute. That don't make no sense. If I have a coffee can on each ear, then what am I going to use as a microphone?"

The man sat there momentarily then answered smugly, "Well, it'll give you something to talk about."

"Why I bother . . ." she said to no one in particular. "So she comes home and starts talkin' about how she doesn't want to eat meat no more. She only eats vegetables, and she's wants to go to college out in California."

"California?"

"Yeah, California. Remember Bill and MaryAnne Coyne? From our old apartment building?"

"Yeah."

"Their son is moving out there, and he's been tellin' her all about it."

"Their son is a crackpot. What the hell does my daughter want to move out to California for? In California, it takes an hour and a half to watch *Sixty Minutes*. Here in Philadelphia . . . forty-five!"

"So I says, go for it." She went on as though he weren't there.

I wondered if they were two crazy people, talking to themselves, who just happened to be sitting next to one another.

"I says to her if that's what you want, then do it." She made a definitive *hmph* noise that I am not able to articulate.

The man followed that with an *eh*-sounding noise, which let me know that although he wasn't crazy about his daughter going to California, he knew he was a powerless figurehead.

"Hey, you're young, I says. That's what I told her yesterday. I told her, I says, go for it! She could go out there, meet some handsome lifeguard, and fall in love."

"Yeah, that's the last thing I need. Some long-haired hippie freak raising my grandkids. Maybe you're the one who wants to go out there and meet some hippie lifeguard."

"No, no," she said and laughed. "A lifeguard is big and muscular. With a shaved head." She smiled at the thought.

"Oh, so that's what you want," he said, waving his arms for emphasis. "One of these days, you're gonna run off and I'm gonna lose you, babe. I'm gonna lose you to one of those college guys. Know what I'm sayin'?"

The woman made several noises of disagreement, but then just gave up and laughed.

He elbowed her and ran right on over her chuckling. "You're gonna go visit her out there, and then you're gonna be da one to come home with some bald lifeguard. I'm finished." He gestured to the empty seat across the aisle, as though the adulterous lifeguard were sitting there. "I can't compete with this guy. He's young. He's popular. He's bald. Hell, he already looks like a big penis."

She broke into hysterics while I did everything I could not to follow suit. But like any good comic, the man in front of me was saving the best for last.

"I'm serious. When you look at that lifeguard, he's got that smooth body and that shaved-bald head, it's like he's a big, walking dildo! I can't compete with that. I'm out."

She kept laughing hysterically and smacked him in the arm harder than any of the other times, trying to get him to shut the hell up.

"Seriously. I'm gonna lose you, babe. I'm gonna lose you to some young, bald lifeguard. Christ, you could use his whole head as a sex toy while I'm sittin' here, rubbing enlargement creams all over myself. I'm startin' to feel silly over here."

"Oh, Paul, you always do a good job . . ." She boasted of his skills in bed, and I launched myself backward as though the seat in front of me were on fire. Before I could extricate myself from my eavesdropping, I had learned too much about Paul's abilities. Eavesdropping is a lot like playing a slot machine; it's hard to know when to stop until it's too late.

Despite the sour ending of the chat, in some odd way, the story about the lifeguard spoke to me on many levels. I would never admit this to anyone, but I found the story about his wife using a stranger's bald head as a dildo to be quite an inspiration. Riding the bus is a rough gig, but Paul managed to find the humor in what was going on around him, and anyone around him was better off for having been there. It doesn't matter if it's a breathtaking view from a scenic mountaintop or your wife's musing about having sex with a bald stranger. The things we see every day shape us into the people we are. Paul was a funny guy, so she was a happy lady. They got off at the next stop, and I could've followed him around all day, sipping coffee and lifting material. If I ever write that novel I've been talking about since high school, I'm going to use his jokes, although it would be impossible to work them into any plot line. Impossible.

The rest of the ride sucked. After Mr. and Mrs. Paul got off the bus, some jarhead with a crew cut sat down in the same seat. He sat there for the entire ride, offering nothing but the smell of cheap aftershave and the back of his head. I was thankful for the entertainment I had gotten from Paul, the wiseass who's good in bed. People such as Paul give this city its flavor, and for those few moments, the bus seemed to run on time.

The bus arrived in Ralph's neighborhood, across the street from the Happy Burger. We got off but stayed at the bus stop for several hours. The location provided us a perfect vantage point of the door Ralph would be leaving through, but most important of all, we had a place to sit down. Every once in a while, a bus would pull up to the stop under the assumption that we wanted a ride, but we would wave it through as the driver flipped us off.

As we observed the city and life going on around us, we did what any two gangsters waiting to kick the crap out of some deadbeat would do. We took time to reflect.

"Man, this psychology class that I'm taking is keeping me up at night," John said.

I thought about throwing out some joke about how John is awake at night because he's actually looking at pornography on his computer, but it been told before, several thousand times. The secret of comedy is to make sure you're not mindlessly inserting jokes everybody has already heard into any situation where they might apply. I caught myself before I said anything, which allowed John's train of thought to roll along. Sometimes it's the jokes you don't tell that save your act.

"First let me tell you the story about Mike." John paused for a moment, looking at me curiously. "How's the music, Manny? Can you hear everything okay? Are they playing your favorite tune?"

We both laughed as I popped the pair of cheap earphones out of my ears.

I liked to wear headphones on the bus, even if I wasn't listening to any music, because I value my privacy, just like everyone else. To put it in other words, I hate people. Sometimes I forget I'm wearing the headphones, and they stay in my ears for the rest of the day. This was one of those times. I get a lot of static over my silent earphones, but it's all worth it. On a city bus, deafness is bliss.

"So I've been thinkin' about a lot of things," John continued. "You know that kid Mike, right?"

"Yeah. I saw him last Thursday at happy hour. That kid's on the level." I remembered when I saw Mike that night, he had his mojo working, and he appeared to be having a much better night than I was. Girls were talking to him.

"Mike's the man. That boy's sharp as a tack."

Both of us had met Mike last fall. He was one of those people you would see all over town. Mike hit every party and every bar, every night of the week, and so did I. I had watched him perform.

John continued explaining his pro-Mike platform. "My man Mike will stay out gettin' drunk until four in the morning, then he shows up to take a psychology test at eight in the morning, on time, and he has to sit next to the trash can in the corner 'cause he don't know if he's gonna puke." John looked at me sternly, as if what he was about to say were deep and serious. "Mike gets an A on the test." He leaned back and relaxed as if he had just unloaded some major news. "You know his cousin?" John smacked me and yelled out in a high-pitched tone that scared the crap out of me.

"Who the fuck is his cousin, and why do I care?" I said. "Make this quick; I'm a busy guy." I folded my arms, although I knew we weren't going anywhere anytime soon.

"Mike's cousin is that shaggy kid who follows him everywhere he goes. You've seen him."

"That's his cousin?" I said louder than the situation warranted. I had seen the kid before. He had sleaze oozing out of every pore of his body. "I always got the feeling that kid would fuck his own mother if she gave him the chance."

"That's his cousin," John repeated with certainty. "His name is Chuck. Mike has a hard time with him."

I got the feeling John knew Mike on a business level, but he wasn't telling me. Damn, I should have thought about approaching Mike.

"It's not an easy situation," he continued. "The person sitting on the couch all day is a mangy piece of shit who never leaves the house, but at the same time they're family, so you gotta deal with it."

I laughed while mentally repeating his last sentence, thinking how it applied to my own life. Irony.

"Hard to believe, huh?" he continued. "Well, check this out first. So I'm taking this psychology class, right?"

"Yeah."

"So there's this guy named Sigmund Freud."

I rolled my eyes. I had left high school years ago. Learning on my own time was not part of my curriculum.

"No, no. Hear me out," John said as he acknowledged my lack of interest. "So there's this guy Freud, and he's got this idea where your whole life is decided by the time you're, like, seven years old. It's not like a fact; it's just something that he thought up, but a lot of people agree with him, so it's sort of like a fact. But it's not."

"It's called a theory," I said with contempt as I wondered which one of us actually belonged in college.

"Yeah. Yeah. I recognize that word. There's Einstein's theory of evolution, and then there's the theory of relative relationships. I've heard of that."

I put my face in my hands.

"So check it out," John said in a serious tone. "So there's this guy Freud, he's got this theory about breasts. I'm talkin' titties, knockers, melons, head bangers—"

"Titties? This is what they're teaching you about in college?" I thought about the allure of higher education, and consciously changed my posture to mimic that sculpture *The Thinker*. I seriously considered going to college to learn about breasts.

"No, for real," John continued. "We should talk about it when we're all wasted sometime. It's deep. It's some major shit."

"Oh, yeah! That's exactly what I want to do the next time I got a buzz on. Sit around and get all deep with you about your theory of titolution." I laughed heartily.

"No, hear me out, homes. So it's like, the breast man, it's how you see life." John gesticulated as he spoke. "Listen to me. Sigmund Freud was one of the most famous psychiatrists of all time. His big idea was that your parents determine your personality by the time you're five years old. The way they treat you is the way you treat yourself."

An ominous feeling surrounded me like the stench of a bean fart.

"If you were a Viking kid, for example, and your mom was this mean, old, Helga Viking lady, and she's got these shriveled-up little Viking tits, and it's cold outside and her tit is all packed up in this metal bra, you would be a little Viking dude wanting to suck on your mom's titty, but you wouldn't be able to because it's too damn cold. So if you were a little Viking kid, you would grow up thinking that life is harsh because you got this bitch mom with these shriveled-up, cold titties that you never get to see. With parents like that, you'd grow up as a pissed-off little kid, and so then when you got older and became an adult, you would go around kickin' the crap out of people from one country to the next. People like the Vikings, man, they would kill kids in front of the parents, and then they would make the parents eat the kids. I'm talking with a straight knife and fork. They would make people eat their kids like a pizza, while the Vikings watched, and then they would make the husband eat the wife until there was nobody left."

"Don't tell Roberto that story." I sat there for a moment. "Wait a minute. Who eats the last person left?"

"The Vikings, man! They didn't give a fuck. They raped, they murdered, and they did all this other shit because the bottom line was that they all had a shitty childhood because when you're a Viking kid, it's just too damn cold to get to your mom's tit and that has everything to do with what kind of a person you are. But if you grew up in Africa, on the other hand . . ." John paused as the topic shifted.

I looked around and noticed the sun beginning to set.

"In Africa things would be much different when you're a little African kid. Your mom is already half naked, and she's got this big African titty and you're like . . ." John gestured with his arms as if he were sucking on a tit the size of a weather balloon. Then he did the Maypole dance around the bus bench. "So you're pumped!" John yelled from a few feet away, showboating as if he had just scored the winning touchdown.

I immediately nodded for him to come closer before the conversation went any further. I didn't want anyone to see or hear this. It was embarrassing.

He sat back down and proceeded with his lecture. "His bottom line—Freud's, I mean—was that your personality is like a piece of clay that hardens by the time you're five, and all of the shit that happens to you before you turn five makes you who you are. It's like your parents pound you into a mold, and after that you're stuck being the person you're molded into." He paused.

I raised an eyebrow.

"So your life would turn out different down there in Africa because as a little kid you got this big African titty floppin' around all day, people are playin' drums, everybody's happy because there's a monster tit for every citizen." He sat there while I laughed. "Seriously, the government has a program down there where if you don't have a titty, you can get like a government-issued tit stamp, and the hookers will honor it like a food stamp." He sat there and laughed.

"That's deep," I said.

"Here's the deal. When you're a little kid, if you see a lot of titty, you're gonna be a nice guy, and if you don't, then you're stuck being a dick. That's the way it is."

"So what's this got to do with Mike?"

"Mike just got robbed by his cousin Chuck two weeks ago. That piece of shit cleaned out the whole house. He took the stereo, he took the television, and he took the computer after he'd been staying there rent free and eating all of Mike's food for weeks."

"What!" I jumped up off the bench, full of fury, wanting to fight somebody. I looked around the area to see if Chuck happened to be on the block. It was random and a long shot, but I wanted blood. Actions such as his are unacceptable, and some people need to have things explained to them. When I didn't see him, I punched the map of Philadelphia bus routes on the wall.

"Calm down, Manny," John said condescendingly. He was always telling me that I blow up too often and it was a waste of energy, but this latest news was more than I could stand. It just didn't make any sense.

"How the fuck could you steal from your own flesh and blood? There's a million ways to hustle money out of these college punks!" I declared, full of rage. John had things to say, but I had to explain why I flipped my lid. I felt justified. "Shit, for a man with no ethics, he could've sold fake drugs. Taken fake bets. Hell, set up a fucking fake charity, for Pete's sake." I used to talk a lot about setting up a fake charity for my own benefit, but lately it had slipped my mind.

John started laughing. "That's one I haven't heard in a while," he replied under his breath.

"There was no need for him to do that."

"Heroin," John interrupted me. "Somehow, Chuck managed to feel a need."

"That's no excuse," I shot back. "If you're strung out on dope and you need money, there's other ways to do it. You don't need to steal from the people who already give you everything you need. So you're sayin' that Chuck stayed at Mike's house, he ate Mike's food, and then he shit Mike's food back into Mike's own toilet, which we all know, Mike is the one who cleans the toilet at that house."

"True."

"And then this asshole went ahead and took Mike's stuff down to the pawn shop and sold it for pennies on the dollar. Basically Mike paid that kid to come down here, funk out his toilet, and then rob him down to his Oreos."

"It's bullshit."

"I can relate to the fact that his cousin needed money. I could understand that. I mean, I look at life like anything goes. If you don't lock your doors and you get robbed, then that's what you deserve. If you go flashin' a gold chain on the wrong block, you're gonna get what you deserve." I paused. I was not calming down any. "But how the fuck is Mike supposed to prevent something like that? It's not like you can turn family out into the street."

"That would be nice," John said half seriously.

"And it's not like he can nail down everything that he owns, either." The thought of one family member doing something wrong to another family member was more than I could stand. I stood up but there was nowhere to go. "That fucking sucks because Mike's a smart guy, and he got fucking hustled." My blood surged and my anger reached its zenith. I slammed my fist against the map again, a lot harder than the first time, cracking the plastic frame. "He got fucking worked by some dumb piece of shit who doesn't even have the balls to sell a bag of oregano at the bus stop when he needs money." I paused and felt stupid about punching the map. "Not that I've ever done that or anything." I knew I needed to lighten the mood. I was in the neighborhood to beat up Ralph, not the wall.

"You need to calm the fuck down. Right now," John said sternly. "You know, I don't get you, bro. You pull this move all the time where you waste time, energy, and straight blood on blowing up over shit that doesn't affect you." He looked at me angrily. "Mike's the one who got robbed here, not you. Mike's the one who punches shit about Mike getting robbed. And what the fuck is with you wanting to turn a blind eye to Ralph! Get a fucking clue! You barely even know Mike, and you're ready to kill his cousin, then you're pulling out a fucking Bible when it comes to Ralph. Get it straight. You got robbed by Ralph. Mike got robbed by his cousin. You punch Ralph. Mike punches his cousin."

I did my best to ignore everything John had just said. I looked down and noticed blood on my hand. "So what's this got to do with Freud?" I asked, exhausted.

"It's got everything to do with Freud," he said confidently and condescendingly. "Don't you see what's going on here? Open your eyes, man. Mike grew up in Buffalo and Chuck grew up there, too. It's colder than a Viking's tit in Buffalo, and it all relates to what Freud was talking about. I think Chuck came down here to get back at his family, bro. It was symbolism. I don't think Chuck thought about what he was doing. It was in the back of his mind, like in his subconscious. That's another thing Freud talks about. It was like . . . It was like . . . subconscious symbolism?" John uttered the last two words as though they were a question, and I knew it was a phrase he pulled out of his ass on the spot.

"You got it all wrong. Chuck is a piece of shit. End of story." Once again, I knew I was right.

"No! That's not the end of the story. Not at all. Freud breaks it down on why that kid is a piece of shit. Freud breaks it down on why that kid came down here and stole from his own family. Mike's cousin shouldn't have done what he did, but Freud gets into the symbolism that motivated him. Chuck came down here to get back at Mike because Mike is his family. That kid wanted to make a statement. He might not even realize it, but it's as clear as day. Chuck saw the heroin as that tit he never got to have when he was a little kid. That's what it was all about. It was a pattern. He had been wandering through his whole life like, 'Where's my titty? Where's my titty?'" John stuck his arms out in front of himself and leaned slowly left and right, as if he were a wandering zombie. "And that's what the heroin was at first; it was his tit. Chuck was like, 'Oh, great! Here's my titty!'" John made as if to describe a second monster tit at the bus stop, but I held him in place.

We were Ralph adjacent and needed to keep a low profile, and I'd already gotten the point.

John laughed at his own enthusiasm then kept talking. "But then, when the drugs ran out, which they always do, Chuck felt some kind of entitlement from Mike because he's family. Mike's got such a good life: he's smart, he's popular, he gets laid. Mike's already got his titty. But when Chuck, his cousin, didn't have no titty—or heroin in his case—he felt like Mike almost owed it to him in a sense because Mike is part of his family, and family members are supposed to be the ones who provide access to the titty. That's what just happened here."

We sat quietly for a moment. The cheap orchestra of loud brakes filled the silence.

"That actually makes sense," I said.

The robbery seemed slightly more digestible, but the pain in my hand got a lot more unbearable. I shook it out as best I could, but it still hurt. The pain was bad, but the embarrassment was worse. I needed a diversion.

Sometimes when we're bored and we need to pass time, I talk in a low voice like an old-time radio announcer's, and I go off on a fake news editorial. I do my best to tackle the issues of the day. This was one of those times.

"Well, if you ask this announcer, these are troubling times we face as Americans. We're soiling our children's minds with pornography, and then we're soiling our own minds with better versions of that same pornography once our children have gone to bed." I paused while John laughed. Now that's a new joke about pornography. I continued. "If you ask this announcer, we're all asking each other the same question before ultimately asking ourselves." I took the obligatory pause. "Where's my titty?"

It sounds cool when you spell it out like that, but that was 189 minutes ago, and ever since then, I had been freezing cold as well as bored to the point of insanity. When I left the house, it had been a warm but breezy afternoon, so I was wearing only a T-shirt and jeans. But now the sun had gone down, and it was turning into a cold evening. I had goose bumps on my arms, and we hadn't eaten dinner, so my head was starting to hurt. Little did I know, my troubles were just beginning.

John tried making small talk, but a person of interest stepped into the mix.

"There's no way . . ." he started to say.

"Hello! Hello!" she said as she strolled up to the bench.

I was so embarrassed that my lunch almost made an appearance as well. I wasn't expecting to see her. I couldn't even look at her. It was Becky. She was all dolled up, wearing a designer skirt that looked great in contrast to her normal waitress uniform. Her hair shone with mousse, and her nails had been polished. On a workday she stood about five feet three inches tall, but the heels she wore added several extra inches. It was her day off, and she was looking good.

"Whatchu two guys doin'? I didn't expect to see the two of yous around here." She paused and looked from John to me and back again.

I've had a lot of awkward moments in my life, but this was turning out to be the worst.

She winked at John.

Don't get me wrong, I don't get embarrassed about anything, but I guess it never occurred to me that she actually did something else besides pouring coffee. I never realized that she would exist outside of her work. I glanced over at John. We all do things behind others' backs, but there are certain things that other people shouldn't know about—ever. The fact that Becky saw us here flipped my stomach like no cup of coffee ever had.

"Great. How you been?" John replied smoothly, clearly having no trouble with the situation.

"Not bad." She practically bubbled with excitement. "I went out to my sister's, and now I'm just gonna go home and watch TV." She paused and it felt like an eternity before she continued. "I gotta work tomorrow, so this is like my Sunday night."

"Sunday? Does that mean you got up early and went to church for me? Did you pray a rosary for me?" John flirted.

"Yeah, right." She didn't spend time in church, and we all knew it.

I looked at her then at him before I looked back at the ground. I couldn't believe they were flirting when I couldn't even get my head around her existence outside of the diner. I focused on the cracking of her gum, which rang out louder than the Liberty Bell.

"Anyway, I'm gonna get goin'. I'll see you guys when I'm at work sometime, okay?"

"Nice to see you," John said smugly as she strolled away.

My mind was void of words and thoughts. I couldn't believe we had dodged the bullet that was Becky finding us right across the street from where she told us Ralph was working.

John tried again to make small talk. "There's no way that girl's tits are bigger . . ."

"Hey!" Becky said as she walked furiously toward us, the fast tempo of her clicking heels conveying her newfound rage. So much for that dodged bullet. "Whatchu two guys doin' in this neighborhood?" She motioned to the Happy Burger. She knew exactly what we were doing in this neighborhood. She's the one who practically put us in a cab and sent us over here.

"Look, Becky, it's not what you think." John slumped casually on the bench as if we were all back at the diner, and Becky, our faithful waitress, were hanging on our every word. However, a waitress is like a hooker: unless you're handing her money, she will act like a raging bitch.

"I got a good mind to call the cops on you little pricks, ganging up on some poor, fat bastard like that." She stared us down.

John and I looked at each other and wondered if she were serious. We sat quietly while I prayed for a way to defuse the powder keg that was Becky's rage. I knew all along that she would be murderously furious with us if she figured out what we were really doing in her neighborhood. This was her turf. John didn't care about Becky's opinion one bit because he felt we had every reason to be on the block whether she liked it or not.

I knew Becky wouldn't approve, I knew she would figure us out then chew us out. She used to bring all three of us burgers, and she always knew to hold the onions for Ralph. She liked the guy. Certain people shouldn't know about certain things—ever.

"Yous two don't know the first thing about human psychology, do you?" she asked, her makeup struggling to cling to her furrowed brow.

I almost laughed as I thought of our previous Freudian conversation and the monster tit of life. I knew John got the joke, but he didn't laugh, either.

"You two are nothing but a couple of sleazebag pricks. And by the way, you two don't even know what the fuck you're doing." The gum cracked and she continued lecturing. "Ya know, you attract a lot more flies with honey than you do with vinegar. If you beat up Ralph, then it's over for good. He's just gonna leave this neighborhood, and I'll never show you where he lives in a million years." She cracked her gum a second time to emphasize her point.

I wanted to laugh because she had just settled the argument between John and me about what to do with Ralph, but I didn't dare laugh out loud because I was afraid she would give us a beating that would make us jealous.

When we didn't respond, she couldn't leave it at that. "Christ fucking sake! You sit around and break bread with the kid, and now you're gonna gang up on him as he walks home from work."

"Look, Becky, it's not what you think." John used the same line with the same smooth tone that he had earlier, but he wasn't gaining any ground.

Becky meant business. "It's exactly what I fucking think it is, and don't you tell me one word otherwise," she said matter-of-factly.

John and I looked at each other, and we knew that we had no choice but to sit back and soak in the frothy rage that only a waitress can dish.

"I'll tell you what yous two are gonna do. The two of yous are gonna wait for him to leave his work, then you're gonna gang up on him, two on one, like a couple of cowards, and then you're never gonna see him again and you're gonna spend all day and all night out here freezin' your dicks off and gettin' no money is what yous two are gonna do. If yous was really gonna talk to him, instead of hitting him, you'd be inside bullying free hamburgers instead of sittin' around at the bus station in the freakin' cold when you ain't even ridin' the bus." She cracked her gum again, and I prayed that was all she had in her, but that wasn't the case. "You know what Ralph's cousin told me?" she said in a mean voice.

"I know exactly what his cousin told you," I replied quickly before she could say more. "I don't think that's something that should be repeated."

"Well, maybe it's something you should go and repeat to yourself before you go and do what you're about to do." She stood there for a moment, viciously staring us down. After that, in one of the most dramatic turn-arounds that this announcer has ever seen, she repeated her earlier friendly farewell with the exact same tone of voice she used before. It was as though nothing were wrong and the previous angry exchange had never happened. "I'll see you guys when I'm at work sometime, okay?" I couldn't believe it when she winked at John.

The two of us were plastered against the bench, completely exhausted by her tirade. We nodded in agreement, and she mercifully walked away.

We did our best to forget her after she disappeared from sight, but it was impossible not to wrestle with the subject matter we had just discussed. Becky's words were powerful, and they echoed with a clarity that was undeniable. She had raised an issue that we could no longer avoid, and the unresolved issue hung in the air like a fart from an eight-hundred-pound gorilla. There was a core concept here that needed to be addressed, and once again, I was just the man to articulate.

"So is she gonna call the cops on us?" I asked.

"I don't know."

"Her exact words were, 'I got a good mind to call the cops.'" I paused. "Am I supposed to assume that her mind is a good one? And then am I supposed to assume that a person with a good mind calls the police when they feel it's necessary?"

"That's deep," John said. "But I don't think she's gonna call the cops."

"True. But now I'm sketched out and I'm freezing my dick off out here," I said, quoting her words of infinite wisdom. "How long is Ralph gonna be in there?" I looked longingly at the storefront.

"I don't know. He must be working a double shift or some shit because lunch was over a few hours ago, and now dinner is in full swing." John stood up and shook his arms out as a way to warm up.

"You know she was right," I said.

"Don't start with this shit again."

"No, I'm serious. She was right," I took a moment to enjoy the irony of Becky purveying the same knowledge that college professors spend years and earn degrees acquiring.

Becky knew what the fuck was up.

I continued. "We should be sittin' inside the restaurant, talking to him and bullying a free hamburger out of him. Then at least we'd be hanging out next to a grill, where it's warm. This shit ain't right. How come I'm the one who has money owed to them, but I'm the one sittin' out here, freezin' at the bus stop when I'm not even riding the bus, and now my head is starting to pound because I'm so fucking hungry!" I wanted to punch something, but my hand was still stinging from my previous temper tantrum.

At that moment, almost right on cue, a bus full of people pulled up. We waved them through, but the driver wasn't hearing it. The bus stopped and the driver emerged. We looked up at all six feet five inches of him, and by the expression on his dark face, he could pound us into the ground without breaking a sweat. "If I see you two cracker asses selling drugs around here one more time, I'm calling the motherfucking pigs on you suckers! You got that!"

We nodded slowly in agreement, and the big black man mercifully drove away.

"Now that's a man who's gonna call the cops," I said and stood up. "Let's go get that burger."

"Hang on. There's something I got to tell you. This is important."

"It'll be just as important inside. You heard what the man said. We need to get out of here, right now."

"Listen. Just hear me out. But before we get to that, I can't believe he called me a cracker ass." John rolled up his sleeve and displayed his light brown Mexican skin. "Man, that guy is supposed to be cool, and he turned into a whitey on me," he said, disappointed.

"What the fuck do you mean by that? Why is he supposed to be cool?" I asked sarcastically, although I knew the answer.

"Forget it," John said sharply. "But remember, anytime whitey the bus driver speaks to you, my brother, be strong and decipher his lies. His words are poison."

"Hey, you know what would be funny?" I said. "If some company made a deck of poker cards and they put in 'The Race Card' at the end of the deck. It would make those close hands really interesting because at any moment, the whole thing could go racial." I laughed then got control of myself. "Look, it's fucking dumb to be lurking around here."

"Speak for yourself, Whitey. I never did anything stupid. I just sat here."

"That's debatable."

"Listen. I'll get to the point 'cause that guy's out for blood," John said. "I'm gonna move to Miami in three months. I've been talking with my cousin down there and I'm out."

"Really?" I said in disbelief.

"Yeah, I'm out. Fuck Philly. That's my new line."

"What the fuck did you just say?" I shouted, jumping up. There's nothing wrong with bagging on the city if you live here, but the second he mentioned leaving, I started fuming so hard that I made the bus driver look like a midget. I would kill for this place.

"Easy, Manny," John said nervously; he knew the routine. Spending time with me is like opening a can of soda that just fell off the roof. I could explode at any second. "C'mon, bro. You talk more shit about this joint than anybody I know."

"Yeah, but you don't see me packin' up and skatin' out of here. The ultimate disrespect is to just give up and leave."

"Give up what?" John looked at me blankly. "You're never gonna get it, are you? This ain't a contest, bro. This isn't like, uh, Tuesday Night Fights or something. You got the whole thing wrong, M.C. It's not you versus Philadelphia. It's you versus yourself, homey. Forget about your dad. Forget about the chick at Starbucks who wants to bone me, and for Christ's fucking sake forget about Mike's cousin. You keep punching the city everywhere you go." He pointed to the spiderweb crack in the plastic over the map, and it reminded me that my hand still hurt. "I hate to say this because it sounds totally college—I've probably sat in too many of those classes—but you're only punching yourself, my friend. You"—he pointed at me in a style reminiscent of the bus driver—"are your own worst enemy."

"Tell me something I don't know. You think I don't know that I'm fucked up and freaked out? I know what time it is, but you just don't walk away from the table because you don't like your hand. That's some pussy shit, worse than walking out on a million football bets at the same time. I'm gonna stay here, and I'm gonna win against these motherfuckers if it kills me."

John scoffed at the subtle irony of my statement.

"My money's in this city, and so am I," I concluded.

Both of us were silent as an awkward moment passed.

"What the hell is in Miami?" I asked as a way to end the silence.

"I don't know," he answered. "I know Mike's cousin ain't gonna be down there."

"What's this got to do with him?"

"It's got everything to do with him. Look around, man! We're freezing our dicks off up here, or should I say we're freezing our titties off up here, and we're robbing each other blind." John stopped talking while he surveyed the declining scenery around us, including the fresh spiderweb crack in the plastic. "All this cold weather and all these lowlife motherfuckers stealing from one another . . . You go down south and it's warm, and the chicks are already half naked. It's like your work is already done for you. People are getting laid down there."

"That's about the dumbest thing I've ever heard," I said, brushing him off. "You're trying to tell me that down there in Florida you're gonna have better luck than you would in Philly because the sun makes people nice?" I stopped talking for a moment and soaked in the historic Philadelphia scenery all around us, rich with tradition. "What about the Middle East? How does that fit in to your theory? Plenty of sunshine over there, and yet it's the most violent place in the world. I don't know how to break it to you, John, but people in the Middle East aren't sitting around and holding hands, talking about how nice everyone is to one another. Your theory is way off base. Florida is fucked, my friend. No way the grass is greener down there."

"Yes, it is. The grass is greener and it's stickier, and my cousin hooks up pounds down there for twenty-eight." He nodded with a silent confidence as he spoke. "Remember that skunk weed my cousin smoked with us when he was up here last summer?"

"Yeah." My voice dropped along with my chances of winning this argument.

"What the hell you think I'm going down there for?" He laughed but then his face took on a serious expression. "I'm not saying it's perfect, and yeah, people get robbed blind down there all the time, but the difference down there is that the people who steal from you aren't your flesh-and-blood family. My uncle down there is all right. He's gonna help me out. I'm gonna work with my cousins, and I'm gonna give it a shot. I can't take this crap up here, where my own flesh and blood is constantly trying to get a piece of me."

"I say it all the time. With family like this, who needs enemies?" I chimed in.

"You got that right."

We both forced out a laugh, but in reality it wasn't that funny.

"Seriously, though," he continued. "I'm not kidding myself like I'm moving to Fantasyland or some shit, but when push comes to shove, I can trust my family down there. If somebody robs me or kicks my ass, at least I won't have to sit down and eat dinner with them at Christmas. I can't take this shit any longer. Family is supposed to be the people who have your back, and I'm stuck up here with these no-tit-having motherfuckers. Down there the chicks are already half naked; you're practically home."

"Well, if you're looking to reconnect with the breast, then I guess Miami's a good place for that," I said.

"You should come with me, homes," he pleaded with me. "As long as you got somebody watchin' your back, then anywhere is home. I mean—"

"No way," I said before he even had a chance to finish his sentence. "This place is home. This is my life. Philadelphia. This is home."

John fidgeted and looked around for a moment. I could tell he'd given this a lot of thought, but he didn't know how to close the deal. "I don't see why you don't just pack up, go down there, and start calling that place home. Then you can start complaining about how much it sucks down there," he said. "Think about it. We can move down there together. It'll be more of the same for you. We'll find you some new bars to get kicked out of, and we'll get you a new stripper friend for the weekends. Your dad can still ruin your self-esteem, except it will be once a week and it will have to be over the phone. Down there your life will be like a fresh, blank page, M.C., and then you can scribble profanity all over it. Seriously, you don't got to go livin' in a neighborhood where everyone knows everything about you. Personally I'm tired of this fucking reputation I got. It's like I catch myself doing sketchy shit because everywhere I go, people look at me like I'm sketchy. I'm tired of being Ron's kid. I got all this baggage I didn't pack. I want a fresh start. I want a new batch of girls to screw, and I want a new group of friends to hustle. I'm gettin' laid. Then I'm gettin' rich."

"First you get rich; then you get laid. That's the order of operations. Look, that's not really what I'm looking for in life. You're gonna move all the way down there, and the only thing that's gonna change is you'll get ripped off by a different group of lowlifes and you'll get blown off by a different group of girls."

"Speak for yourself," he said arrogantly.

"Whatever. I'm not looking to go down there and do a bunch of social climbing in a whole new neighborhood. I mean, why would I bother to go down there and meet all these new people? Some of them would end up being my friends, and some of them would end up being my enemies. Why bother to do all of that when I can just love and hate the people I already know? It's one-stop shopping."

"Look at yourself, bro," he said in a tone that changed the conversation back to the usual argument. "You're in your fuckin' twenties. You're supposed to be drivin' around in a new car, screwin' broads and goin' to parties, like it's some movie. Your twenties are supposed to be about making money that you actually get to keep and hittin' pussy that will actually still be at your house when you wake up. Jesus, Manny! Just open your eyes. Just walk away. You're too busy running around playin' Fight Night with your old man to have a normal life."

"Exactly," I said. "It gives me something to do with my time."

"Hey, I'll send you a postcard." He looked at me blankly. I could see him let the subject go. It was obvious he wasn't getting anywhere with me in a million years, plus we had a bigger, greasier fish to fry.

"Now are we gonna kick this kid's ass, or are we gonna sit here discussing Modern Urban Ethics 101?" I asked.

With that said, we sprang to our feet and jaywalked to the Happy Burger. In my head, I could hear the bell ringing. Fight Night was about to begin.

CHAPTER 6

THE DELIBERATION

Fist fighting is the evil twin of lovemaking, and like most twins, they are different yet the same. Strong but opposite emotions such as love and hate bring a storm cloud before the rain. Some people are tuned in to love, and they can tell when love is in the air, while other people are tuned in to hate, and they instinctively know when shit is about to go down.

As John and I walked bravely across the street, I could feel trouble approaching like an old man predicting a storm with his bum leg. Shit was about to go down.

The people around us were strolling leisurely through their lives, but we charged out illegally into traffic, two men on a mission. The wheels were in motion; there was no turning back for either of us, but still I was hesitating to go inside.

I had known Ralph my whole life, and the reality of violently attacking him disgusted me. I had my reasons. I knew some things about him that no one else did. Ralph was like family, but sometimes family needed to be taught a lesson.

We were stalled in the middle of the busy street, standing on the yellow line for an awkward moment as a rush of several cars prevented us from crossing.

I caught a glimpse of myself in the storefront window.

Perspective is everything. Looking at myself in the window, I realized how foolish my actions would look to those around me, but they made sense to me and that was all that mattered. I knew I was making dozens of mistakes, not the least of which was failing to empty my pockets of anything incriminating before making a scene in public, but my head was so full of rage that there was no room left for any rational thought. I just stared at my reflection and clenched my teeth.

Despite my own mixed feelings on the subject of debt collection, and even after sitting through Becky's message of nonviolent solutions, the truth was I was stoned and I just wanted to hit him. Deep down, I knew this was a chance for me to make myself a better person and I was missing the point completely, but I didn't care about myself; this wasn't about me. From where I was standing, approximately twenty feet and seven hundred dollars away from the entrance of the Happy Burger, all I could see was a thief and a debt, nothing more, nothing less. At least that was my perspective, and anyone who doesn't see it like that can go fuck himself.

The traffic paused and we finished crossing the street. Looking at the front of the burger shop, I noticed that some of the bricks were an off-color shade of red. They were different, much different, from the other bricks. I wondered what the fuck was wrong with those bricks. In my mind, I was doing everything I could to avoid thinking about Ralph and the conflict at hand. I wanted to think about bricks.

I pictured a pair of bricklayers opening several boxes of bricks on the day they made that wall, only to find that one of the packages had been spiked with off-color bricks. Since the bricklayers had a job to do, they decided to randomly mix in the off-color bricks throughout the wall; they didn't think anyone would notice. I observed the wall had a checkerboard pattern of red and off-red bricks. The wall would have been perfect if it weren't for that one batch of bad bricks. I imagined that later in the year the bricklayers took a trip to South America and slit the throat of the brick maker who was responsible. After returning home from their murderous vacation, the bricklayers looked at things differently, and they noticed that their own homes had been built using the same off-color bricks. Irony.

John and I approached the entrance, but it seemed to move farther away the closer we got. Seconds stretched into hours, and every step on the sidewalk felt like a journey across the Atlantic. Then I got to the stairs. My limbs went dead inside as I attempted to climb my way up. I didn't want to do this. I had my reasons. The bottom line was that I was just fucking tired and I didn't have the energy to address these issues. No amount of money was worth digging up the past in this manner.

Becky spoke the truth.

I wanted to walk away. I wanted to rise above. But right or wrong, that wasn't the way we did business in Philadelphia.

I kept slugging along until I hit a point where I was too nervous to move my arms or legs at all. The failure of my limbs was troubling because these were the same body parts I would need to kick the crap out of Ralph, and I could barely open the door with them.

But then, almost on cue, John came surging around me and forced the door open like a little kid leaving school on the last day. For a kid who never got any presents, this was his Christmas.

John walked briskly through the door and began opening his arms for Ralph, the same way he had for the David.

Suddenly I was able to move my own arms as well.

I thought about Zapelli's sister lying on her back and moaning during sex; this was the climax.

Through the open door, I could see the first glimpse of the venue for the showdown with Ralph. The dining area was about twenty feet by thirty feet and contained five rows of three tables, and every table had customers. On the right of the restaurant, there was a counter with stools mounted on the floor. The grill and the cooks, including Ralph, were behind it. I recognized his big frame through the bodies shuffling around inside. There were about fifty people in the restaurant, a modest viewing audience.

I knew with absolute certainty exactly what needed to happen in the moments that would follow, and the clarity was a rarity. My fist on Ralph's lip would put his money on my hip. Soon everything would be in the proper place, right after my fist met his face. Poetry.

Despite all the rhyming and stealing, I still didn't want to cross the threshold of the restaurant the same way John did. There was one toxic subject that still needed to be addressed. Mentally I had been ducking out on some important facts, the same way Ralph had been ducking out on his overdue debt. There was more to this story than what the words had communicated, and in my head, I started to drift off and fill in the missing pieces. I couldn't have picked a worse time, but the subject had to be aired out before the first punch could be thrown. Ralph deserved his day in court before he could be prosecuted to the fullest extent of my knuckles.

Becky had brought up the issue, in his defense, when she lectured us earlier, but in my head, I refused to think about it until now.

On the night that all of us graduated high school, Ralph's cousin Gary and a couple of his friends decided it was time for Ralph to get laid.

Pennsylvania doesn't allow prostitution, but despite the law, prostitutes still do it anyway.

Gary told Ralph that some of their friends were coming over, and they were planning to celebrate Ralph's graduation by getting him a stripper, but unknown to Ralph, that wasn't the only surprise the evening had in store. As the night went on, the stripper would turn into a hooker in front of a very captive audience. The hustle was simple, and it was always the same. A sober kid hires a stripper, and the same kid hires the same girl as a prostitute, once she's naked and he's drunk. That way we can all live comfortably and in denial. It's as American as baseball.

The evening started normally enough. About twenty people had gathered in the small and scruffy living room at Gary's house. A nervous but excited Ralph sat in the middle of the big couch, the best seat in the house. He enjoyed a parade of cocktails as he awaited the lady of the evening, whom he expected to ring in the next round of his manhood. Aside from that, it was like any other night for Ralph. Friends drinking, friends smoking, repeat.

Ralph had just left high school behind and was eager to launch himself out into the brave, new world. Back then Ralph knew he had some problems, but he still had positive cash flow and ambitions to go to community college. He wanted a seat at the American table and a slice of apple pie, but he would need a bench seat and there wasn't enough pie to go around. The beauty of being eighteen years old is not having figured this stuff out yet.

The stripper arrived in a normal manner. Her name was Melissa. Back then, before the dope, she was a voluptuous blonde with strong thighs. Her firm breasts would ripple to the beat of the music as she danced.

Her high heels brought her to the middle of the floor. I glanced over at Ralph, who was sweating horribly. The loud support from his friends only served to mock Ralph like a chorus of jeers from an angry crowd of sports fans. Casey was about to strike out.

After dancing to one of the top-forty songs from whatever year that was, the stripper-turned-hooker motioned seductively for Ralph to follow her to the bedroom. His cousin and the rest of the group chanted his name. Ralph stood up and disappeared into the bedroom with her.

One of the guys cranked up the hooker's boom box to give Ralph some privacy.

A few minutes later, an angry Melissa stormed out of the bedroom, fully dressed and muttering curse words under her breath. She dropped the seven hundred dollars the men had paid her and the baseball-sized wad of crumpled-up twenty-dollar bills onto the coffee table. Then she grabbed her radio and stormed out of the house without saying a word. To this day, that's the only time I've ever heard of a working girl returning the money for a job she had already been paid to do.

The gang was speechless. There was to be no joy in Mudville; the mighty Casey had struck out.

About thirty minutes later, and after much pleading, Ralph emerged from the bedroom wearing his best fake smile. He claimed to have passed out for a few minutes after giving the girl the ride of her life.

The disappointed fans looked at one another skeptically before beginning to disperse. Ralph's cherry-popping party was over.

Months passed and summer turned into fall. Ralph grew bitter and fatter. His stack of college applications disappeared along with his sense of which team would win a particular football game. None of his bets made any sense. His foolish picks appeared to be some subconscious attempt to let people know that he was in pain and needed help. He put on a few more pounds and started betting with his paycheck before it was payday. Anytime women were mentioned, he would scoff and say that none of that applied to him.

The whole neighborhood talked about Ralph's downhill slide, but nobody knew the details for the first year because Ralph's cousin Gary kept his mouth shut. Once the level of interest got too high, Gary couldn't help himself, and he began to broadcast the details of the sordid affair in local pubs and taverns. Everyone had been wondering what happened to Ralph, and his cousin was the big man with the answers.

For Ralph, it was like his whole life became a night in that bedroom. He began to see himself as the kid who couldn't do anything right. That summer marked the first time he started feeling a need to play the role of the person he thought the world thought he was. Let me explain.

In my opinion life isn't much different from a high-school play. People get roles assigned by society, and the audience demands that they be in character, or else the play doesn't make any sense. Ralph's failure to satisfy a female forced him to feel that in the play of life, the director had cast him as an incompetent loser. He became an actor reading a script, walking in the footsteps of a stereotype who could never satisfy the demands that society, or any female, would place upon him. That's why after high school he chose a steady stream of dead-end jobs and why he picked the Eagles to win that game. He knew they would lose. They always lose. Rallying around that team has got to be the most pointless activity I've ever seen. The team is exactly like Ralph; they might win a game once in a while, but they'll never cover the spread.

I spent the next couple of years trying to pull my friend out of the dumps, and it was depressing. Back then I didn't know the details of that night, but I had an idea about what happened, and I knew Melissa.

One Saturday afternoon, almost three years later, I took a hundred dollars that I had made off Ralph's poor judgment, and I went searching the neighborhood to find her. By that point in her career, Melissa was focusing more on the hooking and less on the stripping. Her body had deteriorated along with her attitude, and her rates had dropped significantly.

I found Melissa hanging around the bus stop, and I bought myself an hour of her time. I didn't realize it then, but several people I knew saw me doing this, and they told others. Later, when I went out to drink that night, everybody at the bar was asking me about my new "girlfriend" and wondering why my "date" didn't last very long.

It's a big city but a small neighborhood. Around here, everyone knows everything, or should I say, they all *think* they know everything. People thought that I jerked off in that bathroom in the seventh grade, and people were about to think that I was paying a hooker to have sex with me. We're all misunderstood.

The short amount of time I spent with the girl at her apartment had a surreal feeling to it. Her dwelling was a one-room cube with a bathroom attached. There was no furniture except the bed, and the walls were as naked as her body when she worked. I wondered if she even lived here.

She began removing her clothes the moment we got inside her bare apartment. She looked more like a little kid undressing for a routine physical exam at the doctor's than like some chick I wanted to screw.

I asked her to stop undressing, and that seemed to make her more uncomfortable than actually undressing.

Sometimes, when a man hires a prostitute, he doesn't want sex; he just wants female companionship and someone to have a real conversation with.

Believe it or not, sometimes a man just wants to talk. Melissa thought this would be one of those times, and the thought of having a fake-real conversation repulsed her far more than the thought of having paid intercourse with a casual acquaintance. She rolled her eyes and fidgeted like a cat that wanted desperately to go outside.

I guess everyone has different boundaries. Small talk was one of hers. But little did she know, she would be the one doing all of the talking.

Before the night of his graduation party, Ralph was one of the funniest people I had ever met. I always thought that the two of us could have gone on to be the next version of the Blues Brothers. Never underestimate the power of a skinny wiseass who rolls with a crazy, overweight motherfucker.

I knew something had gone wrong for Ralph in the bedroom that night, but he wouldn't talk about it during business hours. Although after a few beers, the picture got a little clearer. During the late summer after we graduated, Ralph began making unusual comments about hookers and sex. It was always when he was drunk, and it was always disturbing.

I had to know what happened that night because Ralph's life had been ruined forever in that bedroom, and I wondered if he were just misunderstood like I was.

I stood in the center of the one-room apartment while Melissa sat on the bed in the corner, cross-legged and confused. She looked at me curiously, and I looked back at her the same. Something had happened. My friend was missing, and I wanted answers.

I knelt down in front of her as though I were proposing marriage. I looked her dead in the eye and asked her what happened that night with Ralph.

Her first reaction was to deny my request. She frowned and shook her head. She said, "No," as assertively as a hooker could, and shook her head a final time before she put her face in her hands. For a girl who was tough as leather and living in a one-room apartment, even this was too much for her to handle.

I continued pleading with her and explaining that I was worried about Ralph and I just wanted to know what happened. I wasn't looking to run a smear campaign against one of my best friends. Honest.

She kept insisting that what went on that night was her business and nobody else's. Then she explained to me that even though everyone looks at her like she's scum, she holds herself to certain standards, and one of those standards is to maintain a level of professional courtesy. What happened in that room was nobody's business but hers and Ralph's. Her ass was for sale, but her story wasn't.

I had a lot of respect for the way she was keeping her mouth shut; it's important in my line of work.

We went back and forth a couple of times before I got frustrated. I stood up and slammed a crumpled-up one-hundred-dollar bill down on the floor in front of her. I took a breath then calmly explained to her that I had hired her to make me happy for the hour, and her job was to do whatever it took to make me happy, even if that meant not having sex.

I could tell she disagreed, but her eyes lit up at the sight of legal tender. Despite her passionate words, she was the one standing around at the bus stop on a Saturday afternoon, selling her ass. She was the one who was desperate.

I knew this fake ethical merry-go-round would last as long as our fake-real conversation. There's balance in the inner city. I explained to her that she owed me a professional courtesy, just like she owed Ralph. Customer service. That's what I kept repeating to her.

Eventually Melissa got sick of the debate, and she left the room and got sick to her stomach. As I listened to her vomit, I took a moment to observe her taste in interior decorating. The only decoration, something I had missed initially, was a group of about fifteen Virgin Mary statues that she had gathered together on the windowsill. It was a cold day, but her windows were open.

She returned to the room and began putting on her high-heeled shoes without saying a word.

I got the feeling this heart-to-heart chat was over. I sighed. I was sure that she was going to hand me back my money and tell me that not everything in Philly is for sale. For a moment, I was proud of her and the gang of Virgin Mary statues in the window. Melissa was a beacon of hope, like a neon Budweiser sign shining through the rain from across the street. I looked at her and wondered what was going to happen to her when she was old enough to be somebody's grandmother.

But then, true to form, she wiped her mouth, put the money in her purse, sat down, and spilled the beans. She wanted nothing more than to get out of that apartment and out of Ralph's head, but after all, she was just a hooker. I knew that deep down inside, she meant what she said earlier about standards and professional courtesy, but she was itching to get high, so her ethics had just gone down the same toilet she puked in.

There was cold November tension in the air as Melissa fumbled with the matches to light a cigarette. She sighed as the last match in the pack fizzled out before the tobacco was lit, so I offered up my lighter and lit it for her the way any gentleman would. After looking at the ground for a long moment, she finally spoke. She was having a difficult time putting her experiences into words, and on top of that, she was just pissed.

The girl explained to me that when she first entered the bedroom, Ralph was like anybody else, a big, sweaty guy with a big, sweaty boner.

I shivered at the thought.

Then she went into detail about the awkwardness of Ralph's attempting to make his way to home plate. She lifted up her head and told me repeatedly that despite what everyone believed, Ralph had no problem getting it up, no problem at all.

The common conclusion among the gossip circles in the neighborhood was that Ralph couldn't pop a boner; he was a lame duck with a lame dick. By the time baseball season turned into football season, the conclusion turned into the truth. And since more than one person believed it, it became a fact. However, despite popular erectile opinion, this hooker was singing a different tune.

Melissa told me the ugly truth was that Ralph was just too fat to position himself at the right angle to get the job done, and he would have to live with that. She explained how they both tried several times to maneuver around his enormous stomach and love handles, but it just wasn't happening. She said that, as the tender moment faded, Ralph became even more nervous and sweatier, and she hit a point where she felt so bad for the guy that she didn't even want his money.

Tears fell down her face as she recalled the evening. She knew what she had done.

I looked out the window and saw the afternoon was fading; soon darkness would be upon us. My cheap phone started ringing loudly, but I silenced it right away without even glancing to see who was calling. This was more important.

She lifted her head again and asked me if Ralph was all right.

I shook my head. I could tell this discussion had really gotten to her as she slammed her half-smoked cigarette down onto a dinner plate she was utilizing as an ashtray.

"I . . . I . . . I shouldn't have done that," she said remorsefully, wiping off the black tears of a woman who wore too much eye makeup. It was obvious she regretted returning the money in front of all of Ralph's friends, but she had been trying to do the right thing. Melissa's job wasn't necessarily to fuck people, but to make them happy. Since she wasn't able to do either for Ralph, she didn't want money for work she didn't do. She had fucked him in a way that wasn't on the menu and was completely opposite of her intentions. In a dishonest world, it's the honesty that gets you.

She cried again.

A woman in tears is like a runaway freight train of emotion. For her, the situation with Ralph was just one more suitcase to throw in the baggage compartment.

I took a deep breath and realized it was time for me to leave.

Glancing at the Virgin Mary statues one last time, I realized it was my duty to save Ralph from his misunderstandings and from his excessive habits. Ralph's soul was going down the wrong path, and this was my big chance to be the ghetto guru who would bring him to salvation and inner peace. In the process I would justify Ralph's existence, thusly justifying my own existence. But more important than any of that, I had to get the kid laid. If he could pop a boner, that meant he still had a prayer, and the Virgin Mary was watching out for him.

I took turns apologizing and thanking the strung-out girl as she frantically searched the ashtray for another match to relight the half-smoked cigarette. I pulled a fresh smoke out of my pocket and lit it for her. Earlier in the day, I had found a purse that someone had forgotten at the bus stop. As soon as I got on the bus, I began tearing the purse apart only to find that someone else already had. The money and the plastic were already gone, but a pack of smokes containing one mangled cigarette remained. I don't smoke tobacco. I wanted money. At the time I wondered what I could possibly do with one crooked cigarette, but I was about to learn that water isn't valuable until you take it to the desert.

Standing across from her, I watched her eyes light up as the butane danced. She was sitting in first class with a Bic lighter and a brand-name cigarette all for herself. She tried returning the lighter to me, but I held up my hand and refused it. I wanted her to have it. I wanted her to have one moment where she owned everything.

She cracked a small smile.

They say trust is going out of style, but every now and again, you can find it in the strangest of places. To this day, I've never heard of anyone who knew the true details of that fateful night except for Melissa, Ralph, and me. If some hooker like Melissa knew how to keep her mouth shut in public, then there was no reason that Ralph's cousin Gary and the rest of the neighborhood couldn't keep their mouths shut about the bullshit theories they had thought up. There are certain things that people shouldn't talk about, ever.

The girl had answered all of my questions, but in the process, she had left me with new ones.

I gazed at her for a moment as she cried and smoked, and I wondered what was going to happen to her later in life, both tonight and twenty years from now. I pictured an old folks' home for prostitutes—now that's comedy. It was difficult to hold back the laughter, but I was standing right in front of her, so I gave it extra effort. After a moment it occurred to me that there is such a retirement home for old hookers; it's called a cemetery. That wasn't as funny.

But even deeper than that, there was the question that cut right to the chase. I knew it was the last thing she wanted to hear, but I had to ask her the one question that was on my mind the entire time. My timing couldn't have been any worse. "What the fuck are you trying to prove by putting two dozen Virgin Mary statues in the window? I don't know how to break this to you—"

My poorly timed words were interrupted by her comical imitation of my poorly timed words.

"What the fuck are you trying to prove wearing a basketball jersey and a baseball hat at the same time?" she said. "Pick a sport, Manny." Her tone was firm and assertive but polite enough to not offend a paying customer. It was a timeless dance. She chuckled to lighten the tension in the room.

I was impressed with her quick wit, but her best revelations were yet to come.

"Forget about me. What about you?" she continued. "You don't even play sports, but yet you're pretending to be an athlete by wearing that jersey right now. You drink and smoke every freaking day while other people have to work very hard to wear those clothes, and you think it's weird that I have statues of a virgin? Let me tell you that I'm no saint the same way that you're no athlete. Everyone pretends to be the things they're not. You do it and so do I."

God damn, I thought. *How did this girl get so smart?* Suddenly I wanted to ask a million questions about her life and her childhood, but after my last outburst, I knew it was time to go. It occurred to me that some questions might never get answered, just like some people might never get laid.

I took the bus home, and when it arrived at my stop, I hit the ground running. It was at that moment I knew I could save Ralph.

CHAPTER 7

THE CONFRONTATION

Looking around in confusion, it occurred to me that I was no longer in one of my daydreams. I was standing center stage inside the Happy Burger, and I was fucking things up.

A sudden lightning bolt of fear paralyzed my throat and crippled my entire body, leaving me speechless and glued to the spot. Ralph and I were standing face-to-face, man to man. This was it.

When a fire alarm goes off, the skyrocketing fear of death makes people run away. I had that fear, but there was nowhere for me to run. My heart pounded like a bass drum, while strong surges of crippling fear boiled my head to the point that sweat flowed out of every pore in my body. Worst of all, I could feel the undeniable sensation of strangers passing judgment on me.

Earlier, when John and I had entered the restaurant, my mind had gotten lost in a story about Ralph, but since then we had arrived at the main event, and I didn't remember any of it. A crowded restaurant full of people had suddenly gotten quiet. Everyone was staring at me, but I had no idea why.

I remembered that when we had first entered the restaurant, a big group of people were waiting to sit down, but John and I stormed past them. We immediately began yelling and making a scene, but I didn't remember much of it. As we went further into the room, I could see the restaurant had a back dining area that was three times the size of the front area. More than a hundred people had been happily dining on the bargain burgers until we interrupted them. The viewing audience had grown substantially. This was prime time.

I glanced awkwardly at Ralph. Sweat poured down his face, and I could see that someone else had gone through the trouble to blacken not just one but both of his eyes. His acne had gotten worse along with his luck.

I wondered if he got beat up by two people or one really pissed-off individual who stopped by twice. This new twist was unsettling. It made me feel like an artist staring at a canvas that someone else had already written their name on. I had no idea how to beat up a person with two black eyes.

All eyes were on me. This was my time to speak, but I had spaced out so hard earlier that I hadn't thought of anything to say. I knew I was blowing it.

As soon as Ralph saw us, he knew that we wanted to kick his ass. Nobody understands you like an old friend. Ralph broke into the silence, yelling that we shouldn't cause trouble because this was where he works.

"Settle down, tiger," I said assertively to Ralph. "John and I were just walking through the neighborhood when John here turns to me and says, 'Hey, Manny! Let's go get a burger. And what do you know?" I paused for emphasis. "Big surprise! Here's Ralph!" I went to the counter with John, and we both sat down, indicating the scene was over and people could go about their business.

It appeared to be working. The volume in the restaurant returned to the normal level.

"Hey, thanks for saying both of our real names out loud, by the way. Twice," John said under his breath.

I cringed, knowing that I had just fucked up. I had forgotten that anytime we were doing something incriminating, our real names were four-letter words. John's fake name was Peter, and mine was Brian. We would be arguing about this later.

Lifting my head, I took a moment to observe the sheer pricelessness of the scene unfolding in front of me. Cooking behind a grill is hard work, and it was amusing to watch Ralph struggling to get things back under control as the dinner orders piled up on him, along with the embarrassment. I thought about all of the stress that I had gone through because of Ralph, and I was glad I took the time and trouble to come all the way out here to settle the score. This is how we do business in Philadelphia.

"You little, fuckin' prick." Ralph leaned over the counter and grunted the words at me before he went back to the grill.

I blew him a kiss as he walked away. Man, he was ugly, but he was also ready to fight. I realized that I had no idea which one of us would actually win in a fight. It would be a showdown between Ralph's nonsexual rage and my battered-child bluff. It never occurred to me that this wouldn't be a slam dunk.

"What are you gonna do? Kick me in the balls like you did to the David?" Ralph said over his shoulder as he flipped the ironically named Happy Burgers.

"Hey!" John interjected loudly.

A slight hush filled the room once again, but it wasn't the same. By that point, several of the customers had gotten bored with our argument, and they went back to their own business. It takes a lot to get attention in this city; people argue all the time.

Ralph looked flustered. It was obvious that we had the upper hand in this theater of burger puppets.

"Hey!" John repeated. "I sucker punched that kid! In his face. I never kicked him in the balls. That would be unethical," he said sarcastically.

"Settle down, guys," Ralph said in exactly the same tone that I had used earlier. He was always stealing my jokes, and I hated it. "I've been meaning to call the two of yous." He spoke with a fake sincerity that almost made me lose my appetite.

I hate it when people pretend to care.

"I got a bunch of money for you guys," he said.

As soon as John and I heard the magic words, we looked at each other and sat up straighter.

I smiled slightly, secure in the knowledge that our time was being well spent. I remembered how all I wanted was to help the cook out and that I'm actually a nice guy. Chef Ralph was a good person in a bad spot, and these circumstances presented an opportunity to collect a debt and keep a friend at the same time, but then I remembered that I should know better than to think like that around here.

"How much do you have?" John said. He was suspicious and with good reason.

"W-what?" Ralph said.

The unusual sense of calm in my stomach was shattered.

Ralph started complaining about all the things that had gone wrong for him in the past six months, and I knew for certain that things were not kosher at this deli. Ralph was not a nice guy.

"How much?" John demanded a second time. His tone and posture remained unchanged during Ralph's monologue. John had heard it all before.

"I can give you guys twenty right now and twenty again in two weeks." Ralph's sweaty forehead glistened.

The many realities of John's Freudian breast theory glared at us. John and I glanced at one another. We felt like nothing more than a pair of walking and talking breasts sitting at a lunch counter. Our jaws were practically hanging on the ground because we were in such awe of Ralph's incompetence. Talking things over was obviously proving to be a waste of time.

I could tell John was thinking about standing up and throwing a punch, but it would not have been wise since Ralph had access to several blunt, metal instruments. It's hard to fuck with the hired help because they're always one step closer to the knives than you are. Always remember that.

I took the moment as an opportunity to lighten the mood. I turned to John and whispered, "Does Ralph mean that today he's gonna give us twenty one-hundred-dollar bills and then in two weeks he's gonna give us another twenty one-hundred-dollar bills?" I laughed while surveying John's body language to make sure he would remain seated.

"I think he means twenty one-dollar bills," John whispered back in the same tone. He was pissed but I knew if he kept playing along with me, he wouldn't start a fight right away. Keeping his mouth shut was another story.

"You gotta be fucking kidding me if you think—!" John exploded with rage, but right on cue, the manager of the Happy Burger stepped in front of us, his stuffed-shirt torso blocking our view of Ralph.

We were forced to look up.

"Is there a problem over here?" the man said officially, looking down on us.

"No. No problem at all." John was initially shaken by the manager's assertive body language and firm tone. He struggled with his words at first, but then he found them. "Tubby over here is treatin' us to a couple of burgers on the house," John said with certainty, pointing at Ralph.

Despite the fact that this was probably going to end in a two-on-one ass-kicking, I still thought it was pretty mean of John to make fun of Ralph for being fat. I looked at Ralph sweating it out across the counter, and I remembered how badly I wanted the kid to get laid. I just wish he hadn't fucked me on money.

"Don't pull that shit," I said under my breath to John. I wanted to kill Ralph more than anybody, but I practically threw myself in front of a bullet when John called him fat.

John looked me up and down then gave me a confused glance.

"That's not going to happen," the manager said bluntly. "You gentleman are either going to make a purchase or I'm going to call the police."

As soon as Ralph heard the word *police*, he sprang into action. "Brian, I'll cover it," he said, cutting his boss off before his sentence was even finished.

I laughed and thought about how my name was supposed to be Brian.

"These guys are my friends," Ralph continued in an urgent tone. "We're kidding around. I got money. I'll pay for them. Don't call the police." His bravery was ironic. All of us wanted desperately to kick the crap out of one another, but the second the police were mentioned, Ralph practically threw himself on a grenade to save us. Ralph's actions might have seemed rude to his boss, but people who break the law tend to look down on involving the law to settle a dispute. Ralph knew this was his bad because it was his debt. If Brian called the cops, they would search all of us when they arrived, and that would be a no-win situation for anyone involved. Two things to remember in a heated argument: you don't call someone fat and you don't call the police.

"You little, fucking prick," Ralph repeated once Brian had nodded and stepped away.

I wanted to blow him another kiss, but I had played that card already. I choked for a one-liner as he took two burgers that someone else had ordered and threw them in front of us. Ralph just wanted us to eat our food and be on our way.

I wasn't sure how to feel about the situation. On the one hand, I was happy to eat, but on the other hand, I realized there would be no happy ending at the Happy Burger.

"Ya know, Ralph, this situation isn't gonna go away by itself," John said around a mouth full of food. He seemed reluctant to swallow the food until the money issue had been resolved.

The piping-hot burger tasted delicious, but the revenge tasted sweeter, and it was best served up cold and proper. Silence hung in the air as we chewed slowly and waited for Ralph's response.

After a moment, Ralph turned from the grill and opened his arms then returned to the burgers. He still had love for us.

I was speechless. After all the threats and harsh words, Ralph was still that same kid who flipped out at the sandwich shop that fateful day. It was an odd gesture on his part, but for us, it served as a reminder of Zapelli and previous mistakes. John and I were caught in the same trap as before.

I looked over at him as he chewed his food angrily. All he wanted was to kick Ralph's ass, and he couldn't have cared less about his ethics, or even about the money. I was beginning to feel the same way, but the sound of Melissa's crying was still ringing in my ears, and it deafened me to John's hard-luck logic.

"Look," Ralph said with sincerity as he wiped his hands off on a towel and walked over to us. "I never planned for things to go down this way." He paused and looked nervously at us. The three of us had known each other our whole lives, but these terms were different. "The reason this all happened is because my cousin brought some sketch ball over to my apartment to buy a dime bag, and three days later, my whole apartment got cleaned out! Dey even took my Oreos!"

My blood boiled as I remembered Ralph's crappy cousin eating all of his Oreos on the day Ralph stormed the sandwich shop.

"How do you know that guy was the one who robbed you?" John asked with less anger and with less food in his mouth.

I turned and gaped at him. John never cared about anything or anybody. This was one of the few times I'd seen him acknowledge that anyone else had a problem.

"'Cause I barely even knew the guy, and then the motherfucker comes into my work and told me he wanted to buy a thousand dollars' worth of weed. I was, ya know, thinkin' of making a little cut for myself." Ralph looked at us for a moment before he continued. "The dude even opened his wallet and showed me a bunch of money. I didn't know what to do. I'm not the drug dealer. 'Member when I called yous and asked you to bring over a case of beer the night of the Pacers versus 76ers game, and then I had to call you back to cancel and tell you it fell through, and then you got all pissed off at me and screamed at me, and then you didn't talk to me for the next three weeks?"

"Yeah," I replied flatly.

Over the years, Ralph and I had worked out a method of talking about drugs on the phone without having to talk about drugs on the phone. We used *beer* instead of *weed*. It is completely crazy to call someone and talk about business on the phone because any jobless motherfucker who owns a shortwave radio can tune in and hear every word that's said. Then they pay you an unwelcome visit in the middle of the night. The irony of not wanting to call the cops really bites you in the ass when your drugs get stolen. They say no man is an island, but every drug dealer is.

"Dat was the time. The guy knew my life story at that point," Ralph continued. "I'd only met him one time, and before I knew what happened, he had knowledge of where my house was. Da guy had knowledge of the inside of my apartment because my cousin brought him over, and he knew that I had access to quantity because I told him I could get him anything he needed. He must have thought I was the one holding all the beer in my house. And on top of that, da guy also had knowledge of my whereabouts when he robbed me because when he came in here to ask me to hook him up, he saw me ask Brian if I could go home early, and he knew there was no way in hell that Brian would let me go."

Someone yelled at Ralph from the grill area. He turned and rushed over to put out the fire. He had left a couple of burgers on too long. He had a habit of turning his back and getting burned.

"That's some knowledge," I said in Ralph's direction. Ironically his story about the scumbag using his information against him made me think back to Brie and her friend at the cookie table in the cafeteria. People at every level of society want access to knowledge that will make them money. The only things that change are the clothes and the intentions.

"Yeah. Whoever robbed me didn't find the stash they were looking for. So that fucking prick scumbag who I only met one time went right back to my fucking apartment a second time and took everything down to my fucking furniture. Nobody did anything. My neighbors saw the guy enter both times, and they watched him load everything into a pickup truck right there on the fucking street, but they didn't know he was robbing me. My cousin said he even showed up right after they left, but he didn't see those punk motherfuckers either."

"Hey, watch your mouth," Brian said as he strutted through the diner with the true confidence of a manager. He slammed the double doors open and walked with pride into the back part of the kitchen.

At that point, a cashier approached Ralph with a question and a lunch order in her hand. They talked about food while John and I continued eating cautiously. Our synchronized chewing kept pace with the tempo of the fast-food atmosphere. The cashier explained to Ralph that one of the sandwiches needed extra onions.

Staring at the salt and pepper shakers on the counter, I considered the concepts of justice and balance. It occurred to me that there are good people and bad people in the world, salt and pepper, nice guys and dicks. Some people like extra onions, while some people demand that you hold the onions. What happens in society is that the bad people who like onions get together and make plans; then everything starts to smell like onions. Justice occurs when good people get together and make plans to take those onions away. Then we all can eat.

The cashier left and Ralph glanced over at me with a distressed look. He was worried about the burgers in front of him, and he was worried how our situation would turn out. I thought about Melissa crying over him that day. All she wanted was for him to be happy, and all I wanted was for her to be happy. I nodded at Ralph as if everything were on the level. Melissa and I had an understanding of Ralph that no one else did, but with John, it was a different story.

"Hey, Ralph, ya know this situation isn't gonna go away all by itself," John repeated. He had absolutely no sympathy for the fact that our money had been stolen by someone else. As far as John was concerned, Ralph's life was nothing more than a number on a page and an inconvenience on top of that.

Ralph looked pissed. He stood up straight, raring for a fight. He had just put his heart on his sleeve while John sat on his stool, passing judgment and looking at Ralph as if he were puke in a dumpster.

The tension rose.

I glanced again at the seasonings on the counter in front of us, and I realized that sympathy is like the salt of debt collection. The tiniest bit makes everything go down a lot easier. I wished that I had explained this to John earlier.

"Dude, you just don't understand what happened," Ralph said.

"Yeah, I do," John said flatly. "You're a fucking asshole. That's what happened."

"Look, Juan. I just told you how things went down, and I told you how I'm gonna pay for it. Maybe if you worked a job once in your life, you'd know what it's like tryin' to come up with that kind of bread. It's not like all of us can suck on your uncle's dick for a living." Ralph turned back to the grill before John could reply. His insult was earth shattering. There would be consequences from those comments. Even Ralph knew.

John put his feet on the floor to stand up, but I held him in place until he composed himself.

"Don't you dare"—John slammed his fist on the counter—"say a word about my family!" John grunted.

Looking around the restaurant, I could see that we had regained the attention of most of the customers and employees, including Brian, who emerged from the kitchen through the double doors. He stood in the back of the restaurant, looking amused, like a parent letting two little kids have it out. Brian knew better than to allow the disruption to the customers, but I think that we had gotten under his skin by that point. It was probably nice for him to hear someone besides the owner yelling. Life is about entertainment, and Brian was bored, so we got to have it out while he folded his arms and watched like a referee.

"Well, don't you dare come into my work and mess with my livelihood!" Ralph's voice crackled like a nervous teenager's. Arguing on the spot wasn't one of his specialties. A few of the working-class folks eating at the tables heard what Ralph had said, and they yelled out in support. Ralph was their hometown hero. He had a job, and they did, too.

"Ralph, look." I wanted to be the voice of reason here, but we all want things we won't get. "This isn't about the money."

"Yeah, it is," John said under his breath.

"This is about principle here," I continued as though John hadn't said anything. "You could've stayed in touch with us. You could've put twenty bucks a week aside, and then this situation would've never gotten out of control like this."

Ralph scoffed at the idea. "Kid, you're smoking crack. How am I supposed to put money away when I drink, smoke, gamble, and I work for an hourly wage?"

"It's real simple, moron. You take twenty bucks a week, you put it in a special place in your wallet, and then after a few weeks when you see me, then you have a stack of twenties saved up for me." I'd thought this through.

"What the fuck are you talking about?" Ralph said. His facial expression was one of absolute annoyance. "Manny, you're talking Greek here. My wallet doesn't have a 'special place' in it." He put emphasis on *special place*, speaking in an effeminate voice and gesturing with his hands. That caricature was one of my standards back in high school. Ralph's mannerisms were shockingly derivative of a style in which I had established precedence. In other words, he was stealing one of my motherfucking jokes. There's nothing I hate more than people stealing my jokes.

The tension skyrocketed.

"Yeah, it does," I replied in a monotone.

"Bull-fucking-shit," Ralph retorted. "In all my life, I've always carried a wallet, and I've never seen a 'special place' in any wallet, at any point in my life. You're a two-faced liar, the same way that you're a two-faced friend. You don't know shit about havin' somebody's back, just like you don't know shit about wallets."

My head nearly exploded. It's one thing to steal from me then run away from me, but don't call me a liar when it comes to something that I know is true.

"It's there," I said in that same flat voice.

Ralph leaned over the counter toward me. "No, Manny. No, it's not."

His arrogance at that moment was more than I could stand. I jumped up to my feet and let loose, screaming at the top of my lungs, "You're wrong! You're so wrong! You're dead fucking wrong! Every wallet has a special place in it!" I had so much more to say, but I stopped talking for a moment and looked at one of the customers who was staring back at me.

His furrowed brow indicated he was in deep thought about where he stood on the issue of friendship, but he was in deeper thought about where he stood on the issue of the special place in everyone's wallet.

I raged on. "You're the one who doesn't know shit about wallets, and you're the one who doesn't know shit about being someone's friend! Not me! The special place in the wallet is right behind the part with the zipper where the change goes!" I pulled out my wallet and slammed it down on the countertop. The bulging piece of leather popped open, willingly displaying the truth. I angrily showed Ralph the special place with my shaking hands. "You see this! Do you fuckin' see this!" I shouted at him as well as the row of cooks tending to the grill. The entire diner was frozen in its tracks, totally silent except for an old woman at one of the tables confirming to her friend that I was right about the hidden place in every wallet.

"Well, excuse me, M.C.," Ralph rebounded sarcastically. "I guess I'm just not the financial planner that you are." He looked over at one of the other cooks. "It's great to be getting financial advice from a kid who names himself after his initials."

Despite Ralph's disrespect and his theft, there was something larger here that was getting my goat, whatever that means. "I didn't name myself after my initials," I said harshly but seriously. Out of all the issues we'd been arguing about, this was suddenly the most important.

"Bullshit!" Ralph yelled.

"Language," Brian said firmly from the back. He was like an umpire calling a strike from home plate. We both glanced at him. Then fair play resumed.

"You're full of it. Your name is Manfred fu—" Ralph stumbled on his own words. It's hard to argue without swearing, we both realized. "You're name is—"

"I know my own goddamn name!" I glanced again at Brian to see if I had crossed the line by saying "goddamn." He nodded and the game continued. "My parents named me Manny Crocker, but that's not how I represent myself. Not at all. The letters M.C. stand for main character because that's what I am. The main character."

"That's what you named yourself after?" Ralph said flatly. He seemed disappointed on a level I could never understand.

I felt enormous shame, but then I remembered that Ralph was the one who owed me money, and I wondered why the crowd was rooting for him. "I call myself M.C. because that's what I am. The Main Character." I declared my identity but with much less pride than I had earlier. "It comes from a high-school writing class."

There had been complete silence throughout the diner while I was mumbling my explanation. Several dozen tables full of people listened.

I felt stupid. I turned to the studio audience and addressed them in a humble voice. "In high school, I tried writing a novel one time—"

"You decided to name yourself after that stupid book you tried to write back when we were in high school?" Ralph said harshly and loudly, interrupting my explanation. "Holy shit, Manny, that novel sucks dick, and the guy who wrote it sucks dick."

John glanced at me with a serious expression. He knew that those were fighting words, and the three of us had now reached the point of no return.

Brian decided it would be easier to hide in the kitchen than it would be to enforce the language barrier so he disappeared.

Ralph continued with his criticisms, unaware of the weight of his words. "I read that book, and it blew chunks. There's something you don't understand, Manny, that you need to fucking learn. It's called symbolism. That book you wrote has references to celebrities who were relevant at the time the novel was written." Ralph paused. "Do you even know what that symbolizes?"

I shook my head.

"It symbolizes that the guy who wrote the book is a fucking idiot who doesn't know what he's doing, and it symbolizes that the guy who wrote that book is just wasting everybody's time, *including mine!*" Ralph stopped talking and just stood next to the grill looking disappointed.

In all the years we had known each other, I had never seen him get more serious about anything. I still couldn't believe that he was the one who owed me money.

He continued to slap me in the face with his insults. "Think about it. Twenty years from now, how is anyone supposed to read the damn thing when you go and make all those nonstop references to a bunch of small-time celebrities that nobody cares about? You're talkin' about O.J. You're talking about John Belushi. The Beastie Boys. Ya' know, god rest his soul, but MCA has passed away in the time you spent dwelling on all this crap. The Beastie Boys are no longer a group! Down the line that shit isn't gonna make any sense. Look at yourself, you fuckin' asshole. You're talkin' about *Children of the Corn* on page one for fuck's sake. Who the fuck has seen *Children of the Corn* in the last twenty years?"

"None of that matters. Not one bit," I said defiantly, springing to my feet and pointing to my crotch. "People in twenty years can suck this dick. Right here. Right now." I declared my intentions proudly as my slicing sword of comedy defended me against Ralph's short-order wit, but then I remembered Brian's warning, and I knew I was breaking his only rule.

Brian had reentered the dining area as soon as he heard the magic words.

I rose to my feet as he approached us. Brian might have found us entertaining, but he still had a job to do.

Ralph's eyes twitched nervously as he watched his boss strutting toward us.

Instinctively I knew that some serious shit was about to go down. I also knew that whatever friendship I had with Ralph was done.

John looked at me urgently. Both of us needed to be out of the door in a matter of seconds.

"Yeah, whatever you say, Main Character." Ralph had more to say, but I cut him off.

"It's Man of Contradictions, you asshole!" I shouted at Ralph.

"Well, which is it?"

I stood there, bewildered. I had never considered, at any point in my entire life, who I was or how I would define myself. I just get fucked up.

Brian had already stepped behind the counter and positioned himself between us, but he wouldn't stop the argument. I think he wanted to know how the soap opera would end, as did the rest of the customers and employees who were also tuning in for the season finale. Brian continued making token attempts at speaking to us in an official tone, but the argument raged on as he and the rest of Philadelphia watched.

"It's Man of Contradictions," I said with increasing certainty. After an entire life of looking in the mirror, I finally felt I knew who I was: I was a guy who didn't know who he was. I had never been more proud. "Open your damn eyes," I grunted through my clenched teeth. "I've been contradicting myself this whole time."

"Whatever you say, Main Character," Ralph fired back. "You think anybody cares about the saga of your seven hundred dollars?"

John punched the counter in anger. Ralph hadn't even acknowledged what he owed John.

I chuckled to myself.

Ralph continued, "None of your small-time, pop-culture bullshit is ever gonna amount to anything. Now you got the characters making criticisms of the book from inside of the book . . . Yeah . . . That's never been done."

As Ralph's comments continued to fly out of his mouth, Brian continued pretending to separate us. We could have killed each other, and he wouldn't have cared one bit, but Brian was supposed to be the manager, and it was important to him that the customers saw him as a man who cared about his job. Of course, he didn't care about his job. None of us do. One of Brian's muscular arms was the size of all of my limbs put together, but for most of the argument, he had stood in the back, watching as passively as a lazy dog, and although he was pretending to separate us, I still had a clean shot at Ralph. Brian's behavior was unusual, full of contradictions. He gave me the feeling that someone was screwing him out of money the same way Ralph was screwing me. The flow of debt collection is like a force of nature, and as a human being, Brian felt he had no real place interrupting the process; it would be like trying to stop a hurricane. We all live in a world full of speculation where the buck stops at the same point the bullshit ends.

For me, the point where the bullshit ended was the ground right underneath my feet.

Brian could see this fact, and he had respect for it. He took a half step back, and it was all I needed.

Ralph and I faced off with a clear view of one another while I tried to think of a witty comeback to Ralph's stream of insults. He got me good. I wanted to return the favor, but I was past the point of communicating with words. In a moment of confusion, I blurted out the first mindless thought that came into my brain. "I'm gonna fucking kill you," I said. It was a classic statement, one that I was certain had never been uttered in the entire course of human history. As I regained my comic instinct, I realized how predictable it was to say that to somebody. I felt bad. I might have been stumped and on the spot, but I could've done better.

Ralph, on the other hand, was only beginning to find his groove. "Bullshit, Manny! We all know da only thing that you're gonna do is to assume the female position in a homosexual lovemaking session!"

Bam! That's exactly how it sounded, and I'll bet that's exactly how it felt.

Once again I was standing in place, looking around the restaurant in confusion. A few seconds ago, I could hear people laughing at a joke Ralph told, and it bothered me, but for the second time, the restaurant had suddenly gotten eerily quiet, and that bothered me even more. I looked at John.

He was shocked. John knew that I had defied Becky's advice and there would be consequences.

The moment after the humorous words had rolled off Ralph's tongue, I had reached across the counter and punched him—hard—in the face. The entire diner was speechless, and so was I. After all the hours of debate and soul searching, after all of Becky's concern, and even after all of Melissa's tears, I just went ahead and hit him.

Fuck it. Fuck Becky. Fuck Ralph. Fuck anyone who doesn't see things from my perspective.

In the aftermath, Brian had made a fast dash to the phone and dialed it. Something gave me the feeling he wasn't calling his wife.

CHAPTER 8

THE ESCAPE

It was at that moment I realized I had the option of leaving. The shit had hit the fan right at the same time my fist had hit Ralph's face, and now there was no way for any of us to stay clean. Brian the manager was left with no choice but to call the police while Ralph swallowed hard and thought about his ethics.

John and I were left with no choice but to haul our asses outside in a big hurry. After exploding out the front door, we flew furiously down the sidewalk like two mice running away from a hungry cat. The police would be arriving soon, asking pointed questions of innocent bystanders. They would take names and write reports. This was one for the ages.

Ambitious Brian would soon be stepping forward to become the public face of Happy Burger, eagerly assisting the police officers with names, physical descriptions, and anything else he could think of. None of that mattered, though, since the fictitious Brian had already sprinted out of the door along with his friend, fictitious Peter.

Of course, it occurred to me that we had not used our fictitious names. Brian had our real names.

We ran out the door and down the street in classic criminal style. Our legs pounded the sidewalk rhythmically while our half-worn jackets trailed behind us like parachutes. The people waiting at the bus stop across the street yelled out in support for us. It doesn't matter what evil you've just done; Philadelphians always root for the person who's being chased.

I was running like hell, but I still found a way to raise my fist in thanks of the support I had just received from the people across the street. I don't care what anybody says; Philadelphia is the greatest city in the world.

About two blocks down the road, John made a sharp left turn into an alley. I followed him. The alleyway, perpendicular to the street Ralph's restaurant was on, ran as far as the eye could see in both directions. As we rounded the corner, my feet slipped out from underneath me, and I landed painfully on the loose gravel. My entire body slammed down hard on the ground. At that moment I knew I had made a mistake when I punched Ralph. I wanted him to get what he deserved and he did, but now it was my turn.

I tried standing up straight, but my knees buckled, and I nearly collapsed. John saw me fall, so he immediately grabbed me, and we hid behind a familiar green dumpster while we took a minute to figure out a strategy. My leg hurt like hell, and it became obvious from John's nervous glances that we would soon be parting ways.

We heard sirens off in the distance.

I was jealous of John and his healthy legs. The harsh reality was that if the cops started chasing us, we didn't need to outrun them; we just needed to outrun each other. The sirens got louder, and I found myself wishing I could be somewhere else. Leaning against the dumpster for support, I wondered what O.J. was doing at that exact moment. I rubbed my leg while I pictured O.J., sitting in his jail cell.

Back in the real world, John and I tried to figure out if the sirens we had just heard were an ambulance or a police car.

I shook my head and remembered what Ralph said about my obsession with B-list celebrities. In all of the years I had known Ralph, I never saw him get that angry about anything. He was mad that I hadn't taken my responsibilities seriously, and it was ironic. I had a job to do as well, but I didn't seem to care too much about my job, either. Ralph had gotten one thing right in the middle of the circus: Twenty years from now, people will not want to hear about celebrities they've never even heard of. None of this will matter.

Stretching out my leg, I took a moment to reflect on my failures. Yet another pair of sirens had entered the block, and the two sirens fused together to create the familiar harmony of the song of emergency.

John was petrified, standing in place like an oak tree, but I couldn't stop fixating on my preoccupations.

I'd never thought it through all the way before, but my job was to spell things out in a digestible format that would stand the test of time. My job was supposed to be everything for me, except I didn't care about my job. None of us do. Basically that's all our society has become, a big gang of random motherfuckers who don't know what their initials stand for and who don't care about their jobs the way they used to. It wouldn't be an accurate picture if I didn't paint the world exactly as it is today.

Ralph can suck it. I know that I'm right. Twenty years from now, people can look back and see a kid who didn't follow the rules and did everything wrong all the time. That's what I'm about.

In the meantime, John and I had to make sure we stayed out of jail.

The piercing sirens grew louder and more numerous. Man, did they call in the whole department? We were no longer observing things from a distance; we were right there in the studio audience, wondering if we would be the next contestants on *The Price Is Right*.

I started reviewing the many possible consequences in front of me while my guts squirmed at the thought of jail food. I struggled to breathe, my heart pounding angrily in my chest. My stomach twisted itself up in familiar fashion, the Happy Burger returning to haunt me. I coughed hard and knew I would need to vomit sometime in the next couple of minutes, but this wasn't the time or the place. Looking back, I realized that I should've chewed a few more bites at the Happy Burger and thrown one less punch. One of these days, I'm going to learn the secret to not getting thrown out of a place where hot food and beverages are being served. I wonder if that's why I'm skinny and Ralph is fat.

John pressed himself back against the wall as hard as he could. His Adam's apple protruded excessively from his neck, and his eyes bugged out of his head. Things were happening fast, and we found ourselves looking down the barrel of a jailhouse gun.

I had spaced out the whole time.

Once again the problem was my fault, and once again the solution was my responsibility. I shook my leg back into shape as my mind went through possible outcomes. The best-case scenario was for both of us to skate off, scot free, and I needed to be the one to make that happen. After taking a moment to think it over, I immediately saw a flash of myself walking briskly and alone then ducking into a local eatery, where I would casually order better food and hope for better luck. John would do the same thing, except in a different direction and at a different restaurant. The police would be looking for a group of two perpetrators instead of two lone wolves, so two different diners would be the perfect place for two different individuals to hide. Another advantage of that plan was that the police would be looking in the places where people normally hide, such as alleys and bus stops. They would never think that we had the balls to be sitting casually in a restaurant, eating onion rings in plain sight. I could call a taxi while I ate a legitimate meal. Jail wasn't part of the plan.

I turned to John to share my plan. We would divide and conquer. My plan was strong, and I knew it would work, but every now and again fate presents you with circumstances that change your plans. I had planned on Ralph's paying me back, but he stiffed me. Earlier, John and I had made plans not to use force on this one, but I had punched Ralph, and that changed our plans. After all of that, I had just made plans for both of us to make solo getaways, complete with hot meals, but shit happens.

The officer's flashlight blinded and frightened us. I felt naked and exposed. He stood in the alley, and I knew his bright light displayed me as the bottom feeder I was. He told us to freeze in a harsh, loud tone while I nearly shit my pants. There he was. The Man. The Fuzz. Johnny Law. The cop stood in front of us, larger than life with his broad, muscular shoulders and his clean, angular face.

Earlier I was certain that when the police arrived, they would stay in their heated cars, driving slowly around the neighborhood in a half-hearted effort to find us with a searchlight. That's what they always do, and that's why we always get away, but not this time.

"Hands up! Hands up!" The cop shouted as I coughed up more vomit into my own mouth before I caught it with my tongue. Luckily none of it went on the officer.

Somewhere I knew Zapelli was laughing; we were about to go down.

The officer took a half step backward to assess the two of us and the circumstances in front of him. He seemed every bit as startled by us as we were by him.

I could tell what happened. The cops had raced over here without enough information, and he wasn't sure if we were the bad guys or mere innocent bystanders.

"What the fuck are you assholes doing back here? Get the fuck out from behind there, and let me see those hands the whole time," he said harshly. His sadistic tone conveyed years of anger and frustration that only a cop can understand. I could tell this guy woke up every morning in a worse mood than the day before, and I could tell he had it in for me in ways I couldn't even imagine.

John and I stepped out from behind the dumpster, feeling foolish and embarrassed.

"What the fuck are you doing back here?" he asked again with more anger.

"Takin' a piss," I answered with confidence. My mind was in overdrive at that point. I could've solved a Rubik's cube if you handed me one. "Tryin' to, at least," I said sarcastically, realizing that I had even myself convinced.

For a moment, the officer looked troubled by my conviction, and he seemed increasingly nervous about his own uncertainty. The facts had been distorted by the confusion and chaos unfolding around us, so the situation was whatever I told him it was. "I don't think we're the excitement you're looking for," I said, nodding my head toward the flashing red lights that illuminated the street a short distance away from us. Luckily for me, cops are dumb. This was almost too easy.

"Shut the fuck up, you stupid, fuckin' fuck!" the officer shouted in my face as he grabbed me and slammed me against the brick wall, the impact disorienting me. I had been wrong about this cop, dead wrong.

Justice happens fast.

The Law knew the truth, and he found it so enraging that his eyes could barely focus on me as he spoke. He was anything but the dumb and passive cop I had been expecting. This guy was mad, so mad that I could see the wheels in his head spinning rapidly in the wrong direction, and I could also see the years of municipal hatred burning in his eyes. The officer looked a lot like my dad, and he knew the deal. He didn't appreciate the fact that we tried putting onions all over Ralph's sandwich.

At that moment it occurred to me that Ralph had made his own sandwich in his own life, and his actions were no longer my responsibility, but none of that mattered to the police.

In this cop's opinion, there were two kinds of people in the world: good guys and bad guys, nice guys and dicks. From where the police officer stood, approximately two blocks and two arrests away from the entrance of the Happy Burger, all he could see was a couple of crooks and a debt to society. Nothing more, nothing less. The showdown between the cop and the robber is eternal, and nothing is more dangerous than a man who has had too much time to think the same situation through.

"You tink I was born yesterday?" the officer said sarcastically. "I saw yous two guys run out of the store because you know what? That's when I was pulling up to eat dinner! That's where I eat every fucking day!" he screamed, staring me down as I looked up at him.

I thought about jail then about drug testing then about my anger problem then about what a mess I would be if the Man got his hands on me and took away the only things I cared about: smoking weed and sports betting. I was like the proverbial round hole, and society was the square peg. This was my day to get fucked.

At that moment, in a surprise move, the officer punched me as hard as he could in the jaw. The force of his fist was awesome. He punched me as though he had just caught me having sex with his wife. The slight taste of blood joined the ketchup and onion vomit in my mouth, and it was not pleasant. Then the officer grabbed me by the collar and threw me back up against the wall with an expertise that was unparalleled.

I thought back to the plumber and his trick about the Heinz bottle during the split second that my head was slamming against the concrete slab because the cop in front of me knew the sweet spot on every perpetrator that would make the blood flow with the least amount of mess or effort. I knew my goose was cooked, and I envied the taste of cold revenge that must have been in the officer's mouth.

"I know Brian. I know Ralph. And I know exactly what the fuck you just did, asshole! Your punk ass is comin' downtown where I'm really gonna fuck you up, you stupid, little puke. You tink I was born yesterday? You try and tell me lies! I'm gonna show you what happens when I have to spend my dinner break—" The officer stopped in midsentence. "Do you know what Ralph's cousin told me?" he shouted, wanting to say so much more, but he was angrier than his words could express. Then he pulled me closer and whispered, "I'm gonna fuckin' kill you."

It was a classic statement, but it held no weight for me. I was on my way to jail.

Glancing at the brick wall behind the cop, I thought about my father. This wasn't good. Little did I know things were about to get worse in ways I could never have imagined.

The glaring lights of the television crew blinded and frightened us all. I felt laid bare. My knees buckled. I could feel the judgmental eyes of millions of people gazing upon me; the viewing audience had grown beyond my wildest dreams. I had just leaped out of the local spotlight and onto the national stage, but for the life of me, I had no clue what was going on.

The officer cringed because he had known all along what was happening, but he had gotten lost in the moment, and he went off script. The cop knew in his gut that he was blowing it because the camera crew, who had just entered the alley, was attempting to film a reality show about the good-guy cops who chase down the bad-guy crooks. The only hole in their script was the reality that this cop's life was nothing more than a kung-fu cluster fuck where he simply punched the crap out of anyone he felt like punching the crap out of, anytime he felt like doing it.

The first few seconds of the film crew's arrival was an out-of-body experience for all of us, even the officer. The cop knew that my freshly bleeding face would contradict the witness statements from the restaurant, and I knew that he knew it, too. The three of us stood anxiously in a circle, like a group of poker players who had just raised the stakes to a level none of us could afford.

I tried as hard as I could to stay on my feet. The dizziness brought me back to grade school, when I used to play this game in the classroom anytime we watched movies with an old-fashioned movie projector. I would stare into the bright white light of the camera bulb until I started to hallucinate. After a few seconds, my eyes would start going crazy, and the reality of my third-grade life would start to look like the shuttering frames of a movie that had slipped off the reel.

I glanced again at the new developments in the alley in front of me. The light from their camera was bright and disorienting, but this definitely wasn't a movie. This was real life. Except this wasn't real life. This was a documentary about real life, and suddenly I was the star.

"Officer, that wasn't me. It wasn't me!" I insisted with a sincere expression. The lights from the camera were so bright that I was forced to squint. I had seen people doing that on cop shows before, and now I was one of them. I wanted to smile and wave to myself, watching somewhere in the distant future.

"Don't you fuckin' lie to me!" the officer snapped back. "I know that was you." His voice remained firm, but I could tell that the sudden appearance of cameras made him nervous. He was anxiously waiting for backup.

I looked deep into the cop's eyes as he was running his mouth and insulting us in front of the entire nation. Although I was angry and confused about being filmed, it occurred to me that the camera crew might just have saved my life. This cop was mad, mad enough to kill me. Everything about me pissed him off. I had weed and a weapon in my pockets; he would soon be finding both. The officer was probably looking forward to relaxing for a quick minute and having dinner with his good buddies Brian and Ralph, but instead he would be unearthing the foreign objects that were stuffed down my pants, all while the scornful eyes of the nation watched. He shouted into a walkie-talkie that was clipped onto his shoulder.

It occurred to me that I still had one ace up my sleeve: my bloody lip. I could see that underneath all of his strong slang, the cop knew that he had made a mistake when he punched me in the face. His body language screamed out in regret the second the cameras had arrived. His once-firm voice sounded nervous, like a teenager on a blind date, and his uncertain questions were getting him nowhere. I knew the cop wasn't excited about the impending consequences, and neither was I.

The officer's goal was for us to be accountable for our actions, but when it came to him and his actions, it was a different story. As we faced off with one another like two poker players, it slowly occurred to me that even though I had been dealt some pretty shitty cards and the deck was stacked against me, this was still anybody's hand.

The officer grabbed me by the wrists and began inspecting my hands for cuts and bruises, but amazingly there were no signs of a fight. In the poker game of life, bluffing is everything, and I was raising the ante of disbelief.

Although I was doing a good job of bluffing as though I were an innocent man, I was merely an actor playing a role on a television show. I knew that at any moment, Brian the manager would come strutting around the corner and flip my cards. Then the officer would see my hand for the bullshit bluff it actually was. There was no way I could win this one, but playing cards boils down to one rule: You've got to know when to walk away, and you've got to know when to run.

With the lights shining and the cameras rolling, I lifted my knee as hard as I could right into the cop's balls.

"Son of a . . . !" The policeman squinted for a second as he backed up, but then his eyes almost popped out of his head. At that moment, the focus of the nation had shifted off me and on to a member of Philadelphia law enforcement who wasn't doing his job very well. The officer's facial expressions went into overdrive, and he reminded me of one of those bug-eyed kids I used to sell ecstasy to.

I stood there for a moment, shocked at what I had just done. John stared in disbelief. For a city that prides itself on brotherly love, our little group was a big disappointment to the national stereotype.

The policeman doubled over, his black eyes open as wide as they would stretch. The cameras were there the whole time. They saw it all.

The cop stumbled backward about three feet, and that split second of confusion was all John and I needed. We glanced at one another briefly before we ran off into the black abyss of the alley while the cameras rolled on with enthusiasm. None of the film crew assisted the officer or ran after us. They had a job to do, and chasing down bad guys wasn't part of it. People start to care a lot about their jobs as soon as they involve doing nothing.

Although John and I knew we would never get away, we ran like track stars. Outside of the light from the cameras, the alley was pitch black, crowded with dumpsters, and only about twenty feet wide. On top of that, we had no clue where we were going. We knew what we wanted, and we also knew that we wouldn't get it, but we still ran off as fast as we could into the void, one foot after the other.

Words cannot express the uncertainty that comes with having blind ambitions. I coughed up more vomit into my mouth.

Less than three seconds later, the alley ended abruptly and opened onto a brightly lit street, stacked with storefronts and neon signs. Luckily for us, the street was busy and crowded with people. We were also surprised to see that there were no angry cops waiting for us at the mouth of the alley, just a pizzeria filled with people going about their business.

We caught our breath for a moment at the edge of the alley before we walked onto the busy sidewalk. The smell of the pizza made me long for a normal life and a normal dinner.

As soon as we stepped off the sidewalk and started crossing the street, I knew that we wouldn't make it. Down the road I could see a police car sitting at the intersection. They were parked in the crosswalk, lights flashing, eagerly looking for John and me in the stream of pedestrians who were crossing. One of the officers was standing next to the car and speaking into the walkie-talkie on his sleeve. I wondered if he was talking to the officer I had just kicked in the balls. I wondered if they were talking about me.

Looking at John, I could tell he wasn't too optimistic about our chances, either.

Both of us were practically shitting our pants, but somehow we found the strength to jaywalk casually across the street as though nothing were wrong. I still had the harsh and painful feelings of pins and needles running through my leg, and I wanted to start limping, but I knew that would be a red flag to the piggies down the block.

Staggering across that busy street, I came to terms with the fact that I had just assaulted an officer of the law. I couldn't stop looking behind me in disbelief to assess both the criminal and the civil damage I had just done. When I had punched Ralph back at the diner, the shit had hit the fan. But when I kicked a cop in his nuts in front of an entire television crew, it was like the shit had hit a fan the size of a jet engine; the effects would be worldwide. There was no way the police would ever let this go. They had us on camera, and they knew our real first names. Heck, I had announced my whole name to a restaurant full of people. I wondered how far Ralph would go to help them fill in the blanks.

Things had gone wrong on a level that was almost unexplainable, and it occurred to me that I was making things worse by running away.

John jumped onto the other sidewalk, and I followed. We slithered off in the opposite direction of the police car, cutting against the grain of tax-paying citizens strolling casually through their lives.

It was then I realized the assault I had just committed was a felony.

We did our best to act casually before we ducked into the entrance of the second alley. John even stopped somebody and asked if she knew what the cops were doing at the end of the street. From a block away, we were nothing more than two stick figures with unassuming body language who just kept walking along.

I had played tag my whole life, but this time it was for keeps.

After stepping into the second alley, we shot through it like two sperm racing toward the egg of freedom. I was running so fast that I thought I might fly, and my sneakers were struggling to stay on the cement with every furious step I took. My eyes had adjusted to the alley by then, and I could finally see the lumps of dumpsters, hiding in the darkness. I laughed as I thought about how it would have been a great time to put on my fake headphones and pretend I was listening to some crazy chase music, as if we were in an old-time black-and-white movie.

Even though John and I had made it all the way across the first street, I found myself wishing the cops would just bust us already and get it over with. The embarrassment and the suspense of running away was killing me, and it was killing my stomach. In my gut I knew there was no way in hell that I could ever live a normal life in Philadelphia, and I wondered what would be worse, a few months in jail or a lifetime of hiding in dark and filthy alleys.

I could tell already that the life of a fugitive is like a cancer that devours a man slowly until he wishes he would have just paid his debt like a real man.

I was proud of the fact that I had fought back, but no matter how many people I kicked in the balls, there were some things I could never run away from. John was leaving for Miami. Becky was going to cut me like a steak because I had punched Ralph. Actions have consequences. I wondered if the best thing for me to do was stop running and give myself up, but as we ran like mice through the maze of dumpsters and fire escapes, I thought about what was really important in life.

I knew right then and there that freedom is the most important thing on the planet. It doesn't matter how shitty a life you have, as long as you can walk around outside, you can make things better from there. I needed my freedom because I still had enemies to fight and battles to win. Surrender was not an option.

I thought anxiously about the cameras as I struggled to breathe. I had just played a role on camera that the viewing audience would see as shameful and dishonest, but those people don't know shit. The only time a camera films a man is when he's down in the gutter. There is always more to the picture than what the television shows. I wondered what the audience would think if those cameras had been there my entire life. Twenty years ago there were no cameras rolling when my dad was raping my mom, and the film crew wasn't around to capture the beating I got on the day my bike got stolen, so nothing I do will make any sense to the viewers because it's out of context, like a joke they don't get. The average schmuck at home would see me as being no different from Malachai from *Children of the Corn*, an ugly character from a movie they never saw. People who watch reality television can't see the forest because they're too busy pissing on all the trees.

As we fled through the alley, I looked at the wall I was running past, and I noticed that those off-color bricks were everywhere. It was like the entire city had been built with them.

When a man runs for his life, he starts to see flashes of that life, and his mission becomes obvious. The art of getting away is nothing more than the art of getting back to the mediocrity that he tried so hard to rise above. Boredom becomes very appealing the moment the wolf starts knocking on the door.

I remembered how great it was to be a scrub on the bus, sleeping safely at night without fear that the hammer of the gods would crush my meager existence at any moment. My life might not be much to look at on paper, but it plays out like a soap opera, and I wanted it back. I had to know how all of this would turn out in the end. The bad guys win every once in a while.

I wanted my freedom.

I thought back to the day when John and I scored our first ounce of weed. A springtime breeze wafted in through the open apartment windows. I'll never forget how good a mountain of drugs looked spread out on the Beastie Boys album. The vinyl was spinning around in the record player while my wheels were spinning around in my head, and for the first time in my life, I engaged in the Saturday afternoon ritual of calling everyone I knew on the entire planet and finding out who needed what. The weather was warm for the first time that year, and I experienced the notorious feeling that comes with selling good weed to bad kids. Even though the ounce was short and we paid way too much for it, it was like owning a brand-new bike, except the bike would pay your rent and keep you bent seven nights a week.

As we ran through the alley toward American freedom, I also saw the haunting image of Juan's substitute teacher with his list of bullshit American names in front of him. It's funny how one person's anger can change another person's identity for life.

I thought hard about the realities of being an ex-con. Just like Juan's teacher, the cops chasing after me wanted to change my identity into one that fit their stereotype, but I wasn't having it. The idea that some cop was going to beat me up and steal my freedom to get beaten up and stolen from was more than I could stand. Freedom is the most important thing on the planet because when you take away a man's freedom, you take away his chances to finish drying his clothes.

At that point we had a mission and an escape route. Our objective was clear. We would run through the alley at breakneck speed and keep running until there was nowhere left to run. Then we would be free.

It sounded great in my head, but when I looked up, I could see that two cops were standing in the brightly lit entrance to the alley, waiting for us on the street. Their silhouettes were unmistakable. I stopped running, dead in my tracks, and grabbed John by the arm.

John didn't seem to appreciate it, but it had to be done. He hadn't seen the cops, and he was heading in their direction with the velocity of a run-away freight train. John stumbled until he stopped. Then he flipped his lid. "What are you, fucking crazy?" he shouted, waving his arms. "They're gonna shit a brick on your head if you—"

Realizing that his loud voice would alert the police, I yanked him in between two big trucks parked in the alley, shutting him up and hiding us from the cops at the same time. I shuffled as quickly as I could into the area in between one of the trucks and the brick wall. He followed suspiciously.

Luckily for us, the cops hadn't seen us.

"Why the fuck are we back here?" he asked furiously.

"There's cops waiting for us on that street, right where we were going," I whispered.

"Shit," he said in a hushed tone.

We positioned our bodies so we were completely hidden behind the tires of the commercial truck. Every single breath I took was as painful as it was awkward. Death stood in the doorway as we fought for our lives, but suddenly I was also fighting a battle within myself, and that became more important. I turned to John to explain myself. Sometimes a man just wants to talk.

"I hope that people consider my motivations before passing judgment on my actions," I whispered out of the side of my mouth.

"You want to talk about this now! What the—? You have got—" The look he gave me made me feel as if I had just killed his mother. He was so wound up that he kept fidgeting. His face may have been turning red with anger, but there were points that needed to be addressed, and once again I was just the man to articulate.

"Becky was right. It's wrong to punch an old friend," I said casually to John, pretending his protests were silent and there were no police standing twenty feet away. This was his day to get ignored and my day to get arrested. "I should've listened to Becky. I shouldn't have hit Ralph." Out of all the consequences I would face over punching Ralph, Becky's wrath seemed to be the worst. Ironically I felt a burning need to rationalize her concerns while ignoring the bloodthirsty police who were chasing us down. "But I didn't hit Ralph over the money," I continued as we stood between the illegally parked trucks. "I realize now that I shouldn't have hit him, but it wasn't over the money."

After a moment, John was finally able to express his rage successfully. "Are you fucking crazy?" In my whole life, I'd never seen him get so mad. "We got the fucking cops breathing down our necks right now—one of who you just kicked in the balls on camera—and you want to take time to discuss your motivations . . . with me." He looked at me sarcastically. "I hate to break it to you—"

"I hit him because he stole my joke!" I shouted at John before I realized I had just raised my voice way too loud. I wondered if the police heard me as well. I almost wanted them to.

John just looked at me, disgusted. His main concern was avoiding the consequences of my actions; I felt a poorly timed need to justify my motivations before the consequences arrived. This was an argument even in the technical sense.

"Becky was right. Okay," I continued whispering in a serious tone. "She had it right. Punching Ralph was the wrong thing to do. But he stole my fucking joke right in front of me!"

"Lower your voice," John said in an urgent whisper. "What the fuck are you talking about?"

"C'mon! Ralph used big words to describe sexually indecent behavior. C'mon! I'm the one who invented that bit. I'm the one who thought it up in the first place. Nobody does that bit except for me. That kid is a fucking thief, but worse than that, he's a fucking hack. He always has been, and he always will be."

"I don't know about that one, M.C. Lots of people—"

"Bullshit! His exact words were—!" I finally caught myself and continued in a whispered imitation of Ralph. "His exact words were, 'Da only thing that you're gonna do is to assume the female position in a homosexual lovemaking session.'" John looked at me with an increasingly disappointed expression, so I continued talking in my normal voice just to piss him off. "I said that to Frank Kelly, in an argument, in the tenth grade, in Mr. Harris's third-period science class, and let me tell you, I killed it with that joke." At that moment, the most important thing in the world to me was that the record be put straight. "That's why I hit him. Ralph was in that class. He heard that joke. He saw it all, and that prick-fucking bastard stole my motherfucking money, and then he had the balls to steal one of my motherfucking jokes, and then he had the balls to use the joke to get all high and mighty about stealing my motherfucking money. That's why I hit him. Not because of the money . . . because of the joke."

"He smoked you with it, too," John said.

"I know. It's a closer. I'm the one who thought it up."

"Did you hear how he said 'for fuck's sake'?" John asked me then laughed, even though it was an odd time for that as well. "Good luck trying to find the origin of that one."

"I know, right." I wanted to say something else, but I didn't have anything to say. It was an awkward moment, but then something occurred to me. "Ya know what? I'm proud of him."

"Me too."

"Ralph stood his ground. His whole life I've been telling him to stand up for himself and not to take other people's shit. He always used to tell me how much he respected the way I told people off, and he always used to tell me how he wished that he could be the same way." I pretended to sob and put my arm on John's shoulder. "Ya know what? I think our little Ralphie is becoming a man." With that, I wiped a fake tear off my cheek.

"Boy that's great, M.C.," he said, scooting away from my arm. "Anything else you need to get off of your chest while we're out here? Can I get you anything? A wine cooler? A douche, maybe?"

"No thanks," I answered seriously, as though his question were legitimate. "But there is one more thing. He didn't have to bag on my novel."

"Oh, Christ. Here we go again."

We shut up as a pair of heavy footsteps entered the alley, moving rapidly in our direction.

I didn't know how it happened, but I had gotten so carried away with setting the record straight that I had forgotten about the cops. We knew how stupid it was to talk in loud voices, but we did it anyway.

The two of us leaned against the truck, petrified of the approaching footsteps. I wondered who it was. The heavy sound the shoes made on the cement led me to believe it was someone official. Sneakers are silent, so I assumed the shoes belonged either to a policeman looking to take us to jail or to a businessman looking to take a piss. Either way, we had a good chance of getting hosed.

John motioned with his head that we should leave immediately, but I grabbed his arm, urging him to stay. His expression screamed in silent disagreement. I knew it would be safer to sit tight because if we ran off through the alley, then the cops would definitely see us, but if we stayed, they might think the alley was empty and move along.

The only problem with that idea was that the footsteps were growing louder. *Thump, thump.* They got a little closer. *Thump, thump.* They got a little louder. *Thump, thump!*

At that point, I knew the shoes were less than ten feet away. With every step of the mysterious feet, another hole was drilled in my theory about sitting tight and staying safe. I pictured that in about two hours, John and I would be sitting in a jail cell and I would be wishing that I had listened to his silent nod. I wanted to sprint out from behind the truck more than anything, but it was already too late. As the footsteps walked up to the other side of the truck, only ten feet away, I could see that a flashlight accompanied them as well. Both of us were squeezed between the side of the truck and the wall of the alley. There was only about eighteen inches of space, and although we tried to hide our feet behind the tires, they were probably visible from the other side of the truck. It was obvious that the footsteps belonged to a policeman, and it was obvious he was searching for us.

"I think they're back here!" a voice yelled. "I can hear those little weasels right back there."

I could hear commotion and what sounded like more footsteps.

"Where do you hear them?" the second voice shouted.

The policeman crouched down to shine the light on the belly of the truck.

"Right back here. I know they're back here." The voice was scratchy and still shaking from the thrill of the chase.

John and I tucked our toes in as the ray from the flashlight danced around us like a strobe light at a concert. It reminded me of clubbing on a Saturday night. If only the officer had a fog machine; then he really could have set the mood. I knew that I could never kick both of them in the nuts at the same time. My wrists trembled in anticipation of the cold, pinching steel of the metal handcuffs. There is no hell that could be worse than the suspense that comes with hiding. I looked over at John. His lips moved silently, and I knew he was praying. There was no doubt in either of our minds that we had been grabbed by the long arm of the law, and there was no doubt that same long arm would soon be shoved right up our asses.

The sudden and piercing gunshots came out of nowhere, scaring the shit out of both of us.

I cringed in fear. I thought I was dead, and this was the end of the Main Character, but then I realized my heart was pounding so hard that I had to be alive. For a moment, I wished I were dead.

At first, I thought the cops were trying to kill us, but the gunshots came from the street, and they were followed by the sounds of people shouting from different vantage points. The cops, standing only footsteps away from us, started yelling as well. Luckily for us, the gun and the person who fired it were out on the street. The flashlights disappeared and headed out quickly, along with the cops. I looked over at John. His face was white and something smelled. I wondered if he'd crapped his pants. Regardless, the cops hadn't seen us and that was all that mattered.

"Let's go! Now!"

I should have felt incredibly relieved, but I realized that no matter what happened, at some point I would have to face the wrath of John as well as Becky, on top of the possibility of getting arrested and doing serious time. At that point I knew I could go no further. Freedom may be the most important thing on the planet, but it's hard to keep putting on a show when the whole crowd is booing you. I had fucked up, and I felt like the best thing to do was to come clean. I couldn't take any more.

John peered around the truck to check that the coast was clear and waved for me to join him, but I remained in place as the burden of moral obligation buckled my legs and froze me to the ground.

I was scared.

The whole world seemed like one big, dark alley that I could never find my way out of until I owned up to what I had done. The fear of the unknown is the greatest fear of all.

"C'mon!" John said in a hushed but urgent tone.

I wanted to explain myself, but even I didn't understand my logic. The main reason to stay was the fact that I had a debt to society that I would have to pay sooner or later, the same way Ralph had a debt owed to me. After the recent rumble, neither one of us was in the right because I had just found myself in the middle of doing the same thing that I had punched Ralph for doing; I was running away. The reality of my own words and my sense of fairness were the glue holding my feet in place. I wondered why I should run away and hide as if I were ashamed, when in reality I was proud of what I had just done. The picture of Ralph sweating it out over the grill flashed before my eyes, and I thought about how all people should be accountable for what they've done.

John wanted to leave, but I wanted to stay and do what I thought was the right thing. I was out of breath and tired of running.

"You go," I said to him. "I'm gonna stay."

"What? They're comin' right back for us, homes! And it ain't gonna be pretty."

"I know," I replied with a false bravado.

"What the fuck are you thinking?" John demanded as he grabbed my arm like a parent scolding a toddler.

"I don't know what I'm thinking," I replied shamefully. "I'm thinking I should just come clean. I mean, c'mon! All the bitching I did about Ralph running away from his responsibilities, and here I am doing the exact same thing and running away like some scared, little kid, running through alleys and hiding behind giant tires. What the fuck is this?" I gestured at the truck we were hiding behind. "I mean, what am I afraid of?"

"Rape. Violence. Isolation. That's what you're afraid of and for good reason. Bro, this is fucking prison we're talking about. Years of it. You just punched a cop. You got every reason in the world to make sure you're not the one getting bent over when this bullshit is all said and done."

I could tell by his body language that John didn't really care too much about what happened to me. The police would be returning soon, and he wanted more than anything to leave me in the dust. Of course, he was the one who was gunning for a fight in the first place, but that's just how the world works these days. It wasn't about hard feelings. It was about survival. The cops were breathing down our necks, and it was clear that both of us wouldn't get away. Life often ends in a dark alley, and John was determined to stay alive.

He gave me one last look, shrugged, and started to leave me behind, but in a highly unusual move, John gave it to me straight. "Don't be a fucking idiot, M.C.! You got it right that everyone needs to pay what they owe, but you owe it to yourself to get the fuck out of this alley right now, while you're still an innocent man. Don't get me wrong, I'm all about settling the score, but you're missing one very important point: There is a razor-sharp line between slavery and a debt to society. If you give them the chance, they'll cut your balls off with it."

He paused as his words mingled in the air with the various city noises. "The one thing I learned growing up is that just because someone is saying something to you, that don't mean that you have to listen. Every time I hear some teacher or some cop trying to tell me what to do, I think of my mom cleaning that fucking toilet all those goddamn years and my dad wouldn't even lift the lid for her, not once. For two decades, I watched her ask him to lift the lid and not one goddamn time did he ever do it. That's not the way to go through life, homey, wiping up the piss of the people that you're too much of a fucking coward to stand up to. Just because some cop wants to take your freedom, that doesn't mean that you owe it to him. The world is a gang-bang, Manny. Somebody's gotta get screwed, but that somebody doesn't have to be you."

He grabbed my arm and stared at me intently. "I should hit you for what you just said right now. I got cousins doing hard time in prison, and you're all ready to start grabbin' your ankles just because things are getting rough. I hate to break it to you, M.C., but you're a drug dealer, you're a bookie, and now you're the one who just kicked a cop in the balls on national television. For fuck's sake, you just shot the sheriff, Manny, because that's the kind of person you are. Deal with it. You owe it to yourself, and you owe it to me to take your bullshit all the way down to Miami and tell people it's a sculpture. That's what success is about."

As he spoke, I thought back to my man Paul on the city bus.

John let go of my arm, ready to leave, with or without me, but he was on too much of a roll to stop talking. "And the fucked-up thing about hanging out with you, Mr. Man of Contradictions, is that ten percent of the time there's a little voice in your head that's telling you to do everything that you're told, and then there's ten percent of you that wants to listen. You're inconsistent. Get over it. Get over yourself. Get over the idea that you're ever gonna have a normal life where you work at a job and live in a house and shit like that. Society is like an abusive husband; that's why we're divorced from it. Never forget that.

"Now what we really need to discuss is the fact that they're after us—both of us. You need to seriously think about what's going on right now." He paused as the truth hit me like sunlight. "Now let's get the fuck out of here!"

I nodded in agreement, in awe of his rather eloquent speech. We crept out from behind the truck and saw a lone figure standing in the entrance of the alley. If the person was a cop, he had seen us and was just waiting for backup. I thought I heard footsteps chasing us, but I didn't stick around to listen.

We ran into the blackness once more, but it was difficult since my legs had grown stiff from hiding. The pins and needles returned to my right leg, but I kept running.

Ten yards later, the darkest thought of all reoccurred to me. I didn't need to outrun the police; I just needed to outrun John. Looking over at him as we ran, I found myself trying to outpace him, despite the fact that technically he had committed no crime. If we were cowboys in the Old West, the two of us probably would have hid out in some abandoned building and bravely defended each other to the death. With guns blazing, friends would turn into brothers, and dying with honor would be the top priority of the day. But this ain't the Old West; things are much different these days. In Philadelphia we play a much blurrier version of cops and robbers. Around here the cops rob and the robbers call the cops when you cause a disruption in their restaurant. Nobody stays in character anymore.

I'm no different.

We emerged onto the dimly lit street to find there were no authority figures of any kind waiting for us.

As we continued into the next alley on the road to nowhere, I realized that if we came face-to-face with the law, it was probably going to be only one cop instead of two. He would be able to grab only one of us, not both of us. In my head, I did everything possible to figure out a way to leave my lifelong best friend in the dust to take the rap for two assaults that I had committed. That's just how the world works these days. It's not about hard feelings. It's about survival. I looked over at John again, and I knew he would agree with me in a heartbeat. After all, he was the one leaving me in the dust to go to Miami.

We crossed the street quickly and ran into the next dark alley. I knew that my freedom was the only thing that mattered to me, and I knew that I would step on anything or anybody to get it, but as I heard John fall to the ground behind me, it seemed I would have my opportunity sooner rather than later.

"Son of a—!" he yelled out as he grabbed his ankle and rolled on the ground in pain.

"You're all right. Just get up," I said with a token amount of concern. I had stopped running momentarily, but part of me had already started to leave John like food for the wolves. There was nothing I could do to help. Life sucks and this was just part of it. I tried propping him up, and it seemed to help for a minute, but once he stood on his feet, it was obvious that he could walk but not run. I kept trying to listen for the footsteps to see how close they were, but in the confusion, I couldn't hear a damn thing.

"Just go," John said, disappointed. He could tell by my body language that I wanted to leave, and he wasn't going to make me stay.

I rubbed my chin and thought about what to do. Then I heard the heavy footsteps again.

We lived in a jungle, and there was absolutely nothing I could do to tame the approaching lion. Survival of the fittest wasn't my fault, but every man hits a point where he knows right down to the depths of his soul what needs to be done, and that's what separates man from beast. You can make excuses, or you can make shit happen.

I crouched next to my injured friend and put my hand on his shoulder. I rose to my feet and I did what I do best. Screaming at the top of my lungs, I wove a tapestry of profanity, insults, and empty threats like no one else in this city could.

"I'm gonna sue! I swear to fucking God I'm gonna sue you! I'm gonna sue your boss! I'm gonna sue your family! I'm gonna sue the city! I swear to fucking God I'm gonna sue you, and I'm gonna sue everybody that you've ever met! I'm gonna take your house! I'm gonna take your car! I'm gonna take your fucking wife, I swear to fucking God! I'm gonna sue you with twenty lawyers, and then I'm gonna sue your lawyer, and then I'll sue your lawyer's lawyer! I'll sue the fucking judge, you fucking asshole! You Rodney Kinged me, and I can prove it in court, and you know that I can prove it in court! I swear to fucking God, you take one more step, and I'm gonna have my dad's law firm shut down your whole police department! You punched me in the face, and I can prove it in court, you prick-fucking bastard!" I had to stop yelling because I was out of breath.

John sat on the ground and goggled at me, rubbing his ankle while we listened to the sweet sounds of silence, emanating from the blackness.

I took a half step backward and thought about what I had just done. I had invoked a power that was higher than God himself. The fear of lawyers and the fear of needless litigation burns deep in all Americans. It's the reason there are no more free lunches. The idea that any of us is somehow responsible for the actions of another scares us down to the very core of our existence. If this were the Old West, the fearless lawman would have chased us down like the rats we are, but thanks to attorneys and high-priced lawsuits, this ain't the Old West.

Law enforcement had become a difficult task since its members stopped following the very laws they were supposed to be enforcing.

I had no idea what just happened. It was possible that the sounds we had heard weren't the footsteps of the police. But it was also possible that it was the police, and the lone officer chasing us considered the massive financial effects of civil litigation on the entire police department. Perhaps he made a judgment call to slow down and let the fish wiggle off the hook because the fish had a good lawyer. Much like the suspense of being a fugitive, for a police officer, there is no hell on earth worse than civil litigation.

John rose to his feet, and he seemed to be moving around better. He was still hobbling, but it looked as if he might be able to limp off into the dark night on his own. The threat of the phantom footsteps appeared to be gone, although I wondered if the footsteps had even been real.

As I helped John take his crucial first steps, I said optimistically, "I think they're gone."

"For now," John replied in a sobering tone. "But they're never gonna go away for good. Think about what you just did. You kicked a cop in his—"

"I'm well aware of what I did," I said harshly, cutting him off. "There's no need to live in the past."

"Well, now there's also no need to live in Philadelphia!" John shouted condescendingly. "They're gonna get you, M.C., whether it's in twenty minutes, twenty months, or twenty years from now. Somebody's ass is on the line, and so is the reputation of the whole police force. You kicked that guy in the balls on national television. This is never gonna go away. Never. The chips are stacked against you, my friend. There's no way you can win. That guy is gonna stalk you like you just fucked his sister."

"That's the point I was making earlier," I said, frustrated. "This is never gonna go away. That's what I was trying to tell you before when I wanted to turn myself . . ." I couldn't even finish the sentence because I realized the sheer stupidity of that idea. Luckily for me, John had a better one.

"This may never go away. But you can." He looked around nervously.

"What?"

"When the deck is marked, sometimes the best thing to do is just to switch up tables. Find a new dealer, so to speak."

"What the fuck are you talking about?" I insisted.

"Miami, you fucking moron, that's what the fuck I'm talking about. You. Me. Seventy-two hours from now, we get on a fucking Greyhound and we get out of here. Forever."

"What!" I screamed, jumping up and down with rage. I thought back to the past five minutes. Everything had happened so fast that it was hard to believe the experience had been real. I looked around, realizing it had been real, all of it, and I could see the writing on the wall.

Freedom is pointless when you live in a prison built of your own fears. It was time to leave Philadelphia.

I put my hand over my mouth. If I weren't such a hard-ass, I would've taken a minute or two to cry. I felt as though I had died in the past twenty minutes, and I wasn't big on resurrection.

Although by that point there was absolutely no doubt in my mind what I had to do. I had to leave. There was no going back for Ralph, for Brie, or for my bike. I pictured a stack of thirty-five twenty-dollar bills. My life here had ended over seven hundred dollars that I would never see. The fight and the cops were still only a couple of minutes and a couple hundred yards away.

I wished I could somehow reach out and undo what had just happened. But as the seconds ticked away and the paint dried, I knew the picture was permanent and the verdict was carved in stone.

At the same time, I knew that despite the new reality, I could never leave Philadelphia. I pictured a map of the United States like the one we had in grade school, and I imagined a dotted line connecting the two destination points, Philadelphia and Miami. I didn't have anything against Florida, but the scariest thought of all was the stone-cold truth that Florida wasn't home.

"I don't know," I said doubtfully. One thing I knew was that wherever I went, I would be contradicting myself. I took my hat off and ran my fingers through my thick, red hair. Yeah, I've got red hair. You got a fucking problem with that?

John shouted at the top of his lungs, "You just kicked a cop in the balls! The nuts! The *cojones!* Do you really think that you have a choice right now!" It was a bold move, but after the mention of lawyers, he felt we were safe enough to raise his voice and on top of that, he was just pissed. "Look, Manny, you can do whatever you want, but in three days, I'm out of here for good."

"It's not that simple. How am I supposed to pack up my shit, settle my debts, and move out of my apartment all at the same—?"

"You don't," he said sharply, interrupting me. "You just go. It is that simple. I've been telling you that I was going to leave in three months." He paused for a moment. "Well, in reality it was only going to be three weeks. Now that this bullshit has gone down, it's gonna happen in three days."

"I don't know . . ."

"I've already thought the whole thing through. The beauty of leaving town is that it's like flushing a toilet. When you're done taking a shit, you just press the handle and walk away. Anything that happens in that room after you leave is none of your business."

"Ralph is my business. That debt is my business." I still couldn't make up my mind about what to do. I could see the logic in leaving town, but the beef with Ralph was still seared into my brain, and it was the feather that tipped the triple beam in favor of staying home.

"Ralph is gone. And so is the money," John snapped back. "That bread is like Zapelli's leather jacket; it's never coming back. When something is gone, M.C., then that's it. It's just gone." He paused, the weight of his words hanging in the air between us. "Grab your clothes. Grab your Beastie Boys records. Grab all your shit. We're leavin' in seventy-two hours, and we're makin' one trip. Paradise waits, Manny. Now let's just change clothes and go."

I felt a small tear begin to form in my right eye, so I turned my head. He could never know. I paced and thought about what to do while John walked around, testing weight on his ankle. Out of all the images that were crammed into my brain, I kept returning to the image of myself reflected in the cop's eyes. I was a loser.

"Let's make it forty-eight," I said definitively while I pretended to scratch my eye. I saw a flash of what the next several hours would be like. I would have to slide around the city in some kind of crazy disguise while I did my best to settle my affairs, but in the back of my mind, I knew there was more than that. I had to hide. The big, bad wolf would soon be pounding on my door. I would have to clean out my apartment in the middle of the night and figure out somewhere else to exist until John and I left town. I lived in that apartment for six years, but I would never sleep there again.

There was an eight-hundred-pound gorilla standing in between John and me, and he was farting his brains out. Although I wouldn't admit this to myself until several hours later, I knew in the back of my mind that leaving town meant stiffing Roberto on the money I owed him, at least temporarily. It was heartbreaking. I had set out on a mission to destroy Ralph, but

MAN ON THE STREET

vengeance has a way of turning you into the very people you attempt to destroy. I hate it when that happens. The sad truth was that after the recent events, I was forced to leave town.

Despite the three-alarm fire that was smoldering in front of me, I still couldn't stop thinking about the look in the cop's eyes. He had wanted me dead even before I kicked him in the balls on national television.

This one was for all the marbles. If I could successfully make the escape, then freedom, Miami, and a whole new lease on life would be mine, but if they caught me, then revenge and my freedom would be theirs. It was like some TV game show. John and I squared off against the Philadelphia Police Department over a studio full of glamorous prizes.

I thought back many years to that one birthday when my dad stole that bike for me and sped off in his car. I felt proud as I remembered the angry men chasing him down as he did all he could to get away. Ultimately not much had changed. We were still just a bunch of kids running around, playing a grown-up version of tag.

John and I swapped clothes in silence. I put on everything, except for the socks and underwear, John had been wearing, and he put on everything I had been wearing. It was an unusual way for us to say good-bye, but it had to happen. If the police had put out a bulletin on us, they would match our physical descriptions with the clothes we had on in the restaurant. They would be looking for a white thug with a baseball hat and a basketball jersey and a better-looking Mexican man in college clothes, not the opposite. The cops would also be looking for two people together, not for two individuals. We had to split up. When we were done with the clothing swap, I looked at John's new outfit.

"You look like shit," I said to John as he laughed.

"Tell me about it. No wonder you never get laid." He laughed while I did my best to come up with a reply.

"Well . . ." I looked my high-school clothes up and down. They appeared strange on a grown man. I wondered what the hell I was thinking. "Hopefully life changes like clothes." I wanted to say something more epic and profound, but verbally I was out of gas. We stood silently for a few seconds, unsure what to say. I was still choking back tears, so I was afraid to talk.

"All right, then," John said. "I'll give you a call?"

"Yeah," I said with fake strength as I composed myself. "We'll talk about bus tickets and shit like that."

"Sweet," he said confidently then smiled. I could tell he was glad to have me along for the ride. He turned to leave, but the moment was too much for him. "Hey, M.C.!"

I turned around.

"You're an all right guy. You can smack people around in my kitchen any day. As long as it's not me!" He laughed, shaking his head. With that, he turned and walked away as unemotionally as he could.

Less than thirty-six hours later, the two heroes sat tandem on a Greyhound bus traveling to Miami, Florida. Midnight cowboys riding off into a setting neon sun.

34426839R00099

Made in the USA
Middletown, DE
21 August 2016